Brian reached for Terry's hand. "Hey, I've got something to tell you." There was a silence, and then Brian spoke, very quietly. "I love you."

Terry gulped. "Oh, Brian."

"Yeah, yeah, I know. You've got somebody else. Rob somebody, that guy you hang out with all the time. But I just thought maybe you'd like to know how I feel about you."

"I . . . I don't know what to say," Terry said, swallowing hard.

"You don't have to say anything," he said, with a tiny half-smile. "I just want you to remember that. No matter what happens."

"I won't forget," Terry promised. How could she?

Other books in the **ROOMMATES** series:

#1 ALL-NIGHTER
#2 CRASH COURSE

Roommates

MAJOR CHANGES
Susan Blake

IVY BOOKS • NEW YORK

Ivy Books
Published by Ballantine Books

Copyright © 1987 by Butterfield Press, Inc.

Produced by Butterfield Press, Inc.
133 Fifth Avenue
New York, New York 10003

Library of Congress Catalog Card Number: 87-90794

ISBN 0-8041-0034-9

Manufactured in the United States of America

First Edition: August 1987

MAJOR CHANGES

Chapter 1

"Hey, Terry! We're over here!"

Terry Conklin stepped off the Greyhound bus just as Roni Davies' red convertible screeched to a stop in front of the bus station. She could see Sam and Stacy crushed together in the tiny backseat waving wildly. "Terry!" Roni yelled again. Terry pushed her way through the crowd with her suitcase in front of her, leading the way.

"Hi, you guys," Terry said, smiling. "I thought I'd *never* get here."

"Hi! How was your trip?" Sam walked over and smothered Terry in an exuberant hug, knocking Terry's green wool beret over her eyes. "It's great to see you!"

Terry hugged her back. "It's good to see you, too. How was your vacation? I missed you—or should I say 'you all'?" She hadn't really realized how much she'd missed everyone until just now, seeing them for the first time since they'd all gone home for Christmas break.

Roni danced up, clapping her hands, her frizzy auburn hair flying in the wind. It was pretty cold, considering this was Georgia, thought Terry. "Happy New Year, Terry! How are you doin'? How was the bus ride?"

"Awful." Terry put her suitcase down and stretched her arms. "I think we stopped at every small town in North Carolina. Not to mention *South* Carolina. I think I could have walked here faster. How'd you guys know when I was getting in?" Taking the bus back from Philadelphia was sort of like getting a scholarship to Hawthorne: necessary to get where you were going, but not something you wanted the whole world to know about.

"We called your mom," Stacy explained, coming up behind Roni. "Hey, Terry, isn't that a new jacket?" Stacy looked at Terry admiringly. "I like the style—and green's one of your best colors."

Terry zipped up her jacket, her parents' Christmas gift. "Thanks," she said, pleased that Stacy liked it. Stacy was known as the resident fashion critic of Suite 2C, where the four of them lived. "It was a Christmas present from my parents." Terry picked up her old battered Samsonite from the curb. "Okay, gang, let's go. I never want to see a bus station again. It'll be good to see Suite 2C. You know, I've really *missed* it."

The other girls exchanged looks. "Well, actually,"

Stacy began, clearing her throat, "we're not going back to the suite just yet. We were planning to go shopping at the mall on the way home."

"We thought we'd pick you up first," Roni added with a grin. "We haven't all gone shopping together since before Christmas. And I need a new outfit for the first day of class." She giggled. "You know, something really eye-opening, to wake everybody at Hawthorne up. I want to get the semester off to an interesting start."

"Like that fire-engine red mini skirt you wore the first day *last* semester?" Stacy asked, arching her eyebrows. "With the black fishnet stockings?"

"Exactly," Roni said, helping Terry load her heavy suitcase into the trunk. "Only maybe more bizarre." With a teasing glance at Stacy, she turned back to Terry. "What do you think, Terry? Wasn't that a great outfit?"

Terry grinned and threw up her hands in mock dismay. "If you think I'm stepping between you and Stacy on a fashion question, you've got to be out of your mind." Roni laughed, and Terry climbed into the backseat beside Sam.

"There, you see, Stacy?" Roni asked playfully, settling behind the wheel. "Terry agrees."

"We *all* agree that *you're* bizarre, Roni. The question is, do you know how to dress yourself?" Stacy asked.

Terry laughed and sat back in the seat. It was fun to go shopping with her roommates, even if she didn't have that much money to spend—listening to Roni and Stacy argue endlessly about what to buy, helping them spend their money on the latest designer clothes, trying on extremely expensive things and imagining that she might actually be able to afford them someday.

"So how were things in Philadelphia?" Sam asked, leaning over. "Did you have a good Christmas?"

Terry shrugged. "It was okay, I guess." She turned to look out the window as the streets of Hawthorne Springs sped by. Actually, she sort of wanted to forget about Christmas. Holidays at home hadn't been that much fun lately. The high point this year had been when her grades had come and she'd discovered that she'd aced all her first-semester courses. Her high-school friends had made a big deal out of it when she'd told them. Seeing her old friends had been nice, but they didn't seem to have a lot in common anymore. Most of them were living at home and either working or else going to school at the junior college. Hawthorne was a long way from her neighborhood in Philadelphia in more ways than one. "How about you?" she asked Sam.

"I had a good time," Sam said happily. "I got to see Jon, and most of my old friends were home. But I was eager to get back. I've gotten used to living on my own; it was hard to be in my parents' house. Know what I mean?"

"Yeah, I sure do." Terry leaned forward. "How about you, Stacy? Did you go to any fabulous Beacon Hill parties?"

Stacy turned around halfway in her seat, laughing a little and brushing her fingers through her short blond hair. "Yes, and they were fabulously fattening. Can't you tell? Even my face is getting fat."

"Listen, Stace, the day *your* face is fat is the day *I* take that bus ride from Philly again," Terry laughed. She smiled warmly at Stacy. She felt very close to Stacy, in spite of her suitemate's wealth and sophistication. Terry had the feeling that the two of them had something in common: they were the loners in suite 2C. "Did you have a good time with your dad?" she added.

"It was okay," Stacy said. "Actually, I came back to campus a few days early. I got bored with parties."

Sam laughed. "Don't try to kid us, Stace," she teased. "*We* know why you came back early."

"Yeah," Roni chimed in, making a quick left turn onto Montgomery Avenue. Terry grabbed the door handle to keep from flying into Sam's lap. Roni's driving certainly hadn't improved any over the holiday. It was what her brother David had always called the "white-knuckle" style. "It's got something to do with a certain guy named Pete, right?" Roni asked.

Terry watched the color appear in Stacy's cheeks as her face relaxed into a grin. "Yeah, I guess Pete had something to do with it," Stacy admitted. "Can you honestly think of a better reason to come back early?"

Terry smiled, then leaned forward and tapped Roni's shoulder. "So tell us about Christmas in greater Atlanta, Roni. Did you manage to survive?"

"Just barely," Roni said, shuddering. "My parents

invited all the 'best people' for Christmas Eve, the
crème de la crème of Atlanta society, including a
bunch of girls I debbed with and their nerdy boyfriends. I had to stand around being polite and acting
like I was having fun. It was really a drag." She
grinned at Sam and Terry in the rear-view mirror.
"But I got even. On New Year's Eve I was supposed to go to a party with this guy who's some sort
of junior executive in my dad's brokerage firm.
Around ten I told him I had this *awful* headache, and
asked could he *please* take me home. Then later I
sneaked out with some other friends. We really had a
wild time, I mean *wild*. We hit every club we could
find, and I didn't get home until six in the morning."
She giggled. "The next morning, the florist delivered
two dozen roses from the guy who thought I had the
headache. It made a big impression on my mother,
anyway." She pulled into the mall parking lot.
"Okay, gang, here we are."

Shaking her head in amazement at Roni's driving,
Terry climbed out of the car. "So, what's our game
plan?" she asked as they crossed the parking lot and
went into the mall. "I mean, are we shopping for
anything special?" The last time they'd come to the
mall, Roni had bought one of those computerized
exercise bikes. It took up a whole corner of the bedroom they shared, and most of the time, it was
draped with Roni's clothes.

"Well, actually, we're going to help Roni spend
some of her Christmas present." Stacy grinned. "Her
parents gave her this *enormous* check for Christmas."

"Naturally, Sam and Stacy didn't trust me to

spend it all by myself." Roni stopped in front of a brightly lit store window. "Hey, what do you think about that? Maybe we ought to buy one of those and put it in our living room. By spring break, we would be ready to hit the beach."

Terry gawked. "What *is* it? It looks like something out of *Star Wars*."

"It's a tanning table, silly," Stacy said, with a scornful laugh. "Haven't you ever been to a tanning salon?"

Terry shook her head. "I've never even been to a beauty salon," she said, laughing.

"Well, what you do is you take off all your clothes and lie down on the table and turn on the lights," Roni told her, "and then you get brown all over, so you can wear your bikini without worrying about tan lines."

"That's the last thing I need," Terry said, turning away with a frown. "An all-over tan."

"Who knows, it may be *just* what you need, Terry," Sam said seriously. "You look like you spent the entire holiday holed up in the basement of the public library."

Stacy gave Terry a suspicious look. "Is *that* what you did with your Christmas vacation?" she asked. "Didn't you go to *any* parties?"

"Parties?" Roni gave a teasing laugh. "Let's face it, gang: Terry's idea of a party is ordering in a pizza at the biology lab on a Saturday night. Three pieces for her, three pieces for the lab mice."

Terry grinned. After a semester of her roommates' teasing about her study habits, she was getting used to it. "Hey, don't knock it," she replied. "You'd study too, if you were trying to get into med school. Anyway," she added proudly, "all those library hours really paid off." She paused a moment for dramatic effect. "I aced *everything* last semester." She looked around at the others, waiting for their response.

"You know, the worst thing is," Roni went on, ignoring Terry, "with all this studying, she doesn't have time for boys."

"Hey, didn't you hear me?" Terry raised her voice. "I got all A's last semester!"

"It's not that Terry doesn't have *time* for boys," Sam said, as if Terry hadn't spoken. She turned to Terry. "Remember the formal at Merrill Place, after Thanksgiving? You and Brian Benson had a good time together that night, didn't you?"

Terry shook her head resignedly and sighed. She'd expected her suitemates to be happy about her grades, and they weren't even paying attention. "Sure I went to the formal with Brian," she said, "but it wasn't what you think. I mean, there's no romance there. We're just friends. I keep telling you: I'm not looking for a relationship with anybody. I'm not ready. I won't be for a long time."

"Yeah, sure, we know," Roni drawled, making a face. "Books first, people second."

"Hey, wait," Terry protested. "Brian's a really nice guy—I like him. And it's really great to have somebody to study with, somebody who's taking the same classes you are. But pre-meds just don't have time to get involved with each other."

"You know, Roni," Stacy said reflectively, "I think

you're absolutely right. Books aren't enough—Terry needs more *people* in her life. She needs to join a club or something."

"A club!" Terry exclaimed, her mouth dropping open. "I don't have time for a club. You guys, I'm going to be taking sixteen hours of credits this semester, and there's my work-study job and—"

"Good idea," Roni agreed, ignoring Terry and talking to Stacy. "But what kind of club? I mean, if she's not interested in boys, for heaven's sake, what could she possibly be interested in?"

Stacy pointed to a camera store across the way. "Well, there's the photography club. Taking pictures has got to be better than working on organic chemistry problems."

"Hey, Stacy's got a great idea, Terry," Roni said enthusiastically, punching her arm. "You could borrow my camera. I'll bet you'd meet a lot of good-looking guys in the photography club."

Terry frowned. "Don't you think I've got enough to do, with my job in the theater department and my courses? I mean, when would I find time to take pictures? Besides, I'm not artistically inclined. I'd be wasting my time."

"You're right, you need something else, Terry," Sam said, pausing in front of a sports store. "Something that would be more rewarding—like exercise. How about the hiking club? I heard that they take really *interesting* field trips. Last semester I think they got stranded on a mountain in Vermont in the middle of a blizzard."

Terry shook her head. "You know," she said, beginning to wonder what was going on, "you guys are really pushing this. Can't you find another way to amuse yourselves besides finding things for *me* to do?"

"Sure we could," Roni agreed, "but it wouldn't be as much fun."

"Besides, it's easier to plan someone else's life," Stacy added. "Don't you know anything, Terry?" Sam stopped in front of a brightly lit department store window. "Hey, look! There's a club that ought to interest you, Terry. It's right up your alley, don't you think?"

Terry glanced up. Neiman's window was decorated like a classroom, with an old-fashioned rolltop desk and a big blackboard. A mannequin sat at the desk with a stack of books piled in front of her. She was wearing a pleated plaid skirt and a distinctive green blazer, with the imposing Honor Board silver crest on the top right-hand pocket. In big chalk letters, the words "Congratulations, New Honor Board Members" had been printed on the blackboard.

"Yeah, sure, it interests me," Terry said, taking another look at the mannequin. "I'd love to be on the Honor Board. But I—"

"Well what are we waiting for?!" Roni interrupted in a determined voice. "If Terry's interested in Honor Board, that's *exactly* the group she needs to belong to." She grabbed Terry's arm. "Come on. You've got to get one of those green blazers. That way you won't feel left out when you go to the meetings."

"Hey, wait!" Terry objected, standing ground.

"Roni, it doesn't work that way. You have to be *elected* to Honor Board. Some professor has to nominate you and then they go by your grade point average and teachers' recommendations—stuff like that. It's a very exclusive group."

"The more exclusive, the better," Stacy commented. "Come on, everybody. If Terry wants that green blazer, she should have it, right? You know what they say: Time's a-wasting."

"Sam," Terry protested, dragging her heels and trying to turn away, "stop them! Please?"

Sam shrugged helplessly. "You know what they're like when they get an idea in their heads." She sighed. "Especially when it has to do with clothes or money." She followed behind as they pulled Terry into the store. "Anyway, maybe they're right. I still think you ought to be getting more exercise, but I guess you'd probably like Honor Board better than Hiking Club."

"We'd like to see an Honor Board blazer," Roni told the salesclerk firmly, "in a size twelve."

"Why don't we try a size ten instead?" Stacy suggested. "I think a twelve would be too big across the shoulders."

"Listen," Terry whispered. "Please don't embarrass me any more. Let's just get out of here. I'm not a member of Honor Board! I can't—"

The salesclerk took a blazer off the rack and handed it to Roni with a concerned frown. "You know," she said, "that these blazers *are* reserved to members of Honor Board. They're very distinctive, and—"

"Oh, that's okay," Roni said, taking the blazer off its hanger. "We're just playing a little game, that's all." Holding out the blazer, she turned to Terry. "Now then, it won't hurt to try it on, will it?"

"Come on, Terry," Stacy urged. "Give me your jacket. Let's just see how it looks."

Terry heaved an exasperated sigh. She might as well go along with their joke, whatever it was. She thrust her arms into the sleeves of the blazer and Roni settled it on her shoulders. Then she looked into the mirror and to her surprise, a girl with beautiful shining eyes, wearing the Honor Board blazer, looked back at her. The girl in the mirror looked exactly the way she had always wanted to look: successful and self-assured, proud of everything she had achieved. That was the great thing about mirrors, Terry thought. They only reflected images. She turned back to her roommates and began to take the blazer off.

"Hey, what's the matter?" Sam asked, stopping her. "Don't you like it?"

Terry bit her lip. "Of *course* I like it," she said. Did they know that she actually *coveted* the green blazer, with its silver insignia glittering on the pocket? "But I can't have it. Only members of Honor Board—"

The girls glanced at one another. "Hey, no problem Terry," Roni said, her green eyes dancing. "You *are* a member of Honor Board."

"Really, Roni," Terry said with a sigh. "Don't you think this has gone far enough? I don't think it's that funny."

"But you *are* a member," Stacy said. She straightened the sleeve of the green blazer. "Or at least you will be, after the initiation. Show her, Sam."

With a wide grin, Sam opened her purse and took out an envelope that bore the Honor Board insignia. "Here's your invitation," she said, handing the envelope to Terry.

Terry stared at the envelope. "Are you serious?" she asked, looking from one friend to the other. "What's going on here? What is this?"

"It's just what Sam says it is," Roni replied. "An invitation to be on the Honor Board."

"We didn't open it," Stacy added hurriedly, with a glance at Roni. "When the president of Honor Board brought it over this morning, she told us what it was. The initiation is next week."

Her fingers shaking, Terry opened the envelope and read the elegantly engraved card that invited her to be a member of Honor Board. "I can't believe this is happening to me," she said quietly. A single tear ran down her cheek.

"Well, *I* can," Sam said, giving Terry a quick hug. "We're all really proud of you, Terry. Even if you do make us look bad."

"I don't care about *rooming* with an Honor Board member. Just so long as I don't turn into a geek by osmosis or something," Roni laughed. "Congratulations, Miss Conklin. Now will you please stop burning the night oil?"

"Thanks, Roni." Terry began to calm down a little, but she was still trying not to cry, she was so happy. "You guys set this whole thing up, didn't you?" she asked. "I mean, you planned it all from the beginning, after you found out about the invitation. You called Mom to find out what time to pick me up, you brought me to the mall, you went on with that ridiculous nonsense about joining a club, and then you dragged me in here."

"We sure did," Roni nodded complacently. "We planned it down to the very last detail. It was a pleasure." She nudged Stacy with a giggle. "We really had her going, didn't we, Stace?"

The salesclerk stepped forward. "Have you decided about the blazer?"

"Yes," Roni said. "We'll take it."

"Hey, wait," Terry said, looking down at the price tag. Sixty dollars. "I mean, just because I'm a member of Honor Board doesn't mean I *have* to buy the blazer." She began to take it off. "I'm afraid I can't afford it right now," she said to the clerk. "Maybe in a couple of months."

"Excuse me, but don't bother with a box," Stacy spoke up. "She'll wear it."

The clerk rolled her eyes. "But I thought she just said . . ."

"Never mind her. We're paying for it," Sam said, opening her billfold and counting out two tens.

"That's right," Stacy said, pulling her clutch purse out of her bag.

"Here's my share," Roni said, "and some extra for the tax."

Terry looked at them. "Hey, I can't let you guys buy me something as expensive as this."

"Who says you can't?" Roni asked playfully. "We want to get it for you. Don't complain too much or we'll change our minds. You know how fickle we southern girls can be." She grinned.

"Why don't you call it a belated Christmas present?" Stacy suggested, throwing her arm around Terry's shoulders.

"Or an early birthday present," Sam added. "Or a thank-you for all the terrific things you've done for *us* in the past few months."

Terry looked at them all, and then down at the blazer. "Green *is* a perfect color," she said.

Chapter 2

Terry sat at her desk staring at the sheet of paper in front of her, still mostly blank. She was trying to write her parents a letter, to tell them about being elected to the Board, and about her suitemates' gift and how great it was to be back at school. She wasn't having much luck, though. It was as hard to write to her parents as it was to *talk* to them. They'd been so hard to deal with since her brother David had died. She wished she could share her happiness now with David—or her pain at not being able to with her parents.

But they never wanted to talk about David. Terry didn't like thinking about him being dead, either, but that wasn't going to change anything. Sooner or later they'd have to face the fact that he was gone. Terry couldn't believe it sometimes. David—brilliant, dedicated, handsome, sweet David—was dead, killed by a drunk driver two years ago. She shook her head, trying not to think about it.

Roni suddenly burst into the bedroom. "Hi, y'all. Studying again?" She shook open a plastic bag and a half-dozen cassette tapes fell out onto the bedspread.

"Hey, I've got some really great new tapes," she said, pulling off her black leather jacket and turning on the stereo on the shelf over her bed. "Want to listen to a couple?"

Terry sighed. "No thanks." Roni's idea of great music usually meant listening to Southern rock or pop music as loud as possible. Terry wasn't really in the mood for that now.

Roni turned around. "Are you okay?" she asked.

"Yeah, I'm okay. Don't mind me."

"Hey." Roni came to the desk and put her arm over Terry's shoulder. "Is something wrong?"

Terry shook her head. She'd mentioned David to the girls, back in September. But after she'd told them the basic story, she hadn't brought up the subject again, and neither had they. That was the way she preferred it.

"No, nothing's wrong," Terry said. She picked up her new comparative anatomy book and opened it at random, staring blankly at the page.

"You know," Roni said, flopping down on Terry's bed, "sometimes I don't get you. Remember when Stacy was having all that trouble with her studying and her parents and eating? You were the one who kept saying that she ought to *talk* about things, that it'd be a lot better if she didn't keep it all bottled up inside." Roni turned over on her stomach and propped her chin on her hands. "Stacy always says how glad she is that she took your advice. So how come you never tell anybody what's bothering *you*?"

Terry shut the book. "Maybe because nothing's bothering me," she said, trying to make it sound light. She glanced up at the blazer. "What could be bothering me? I've just made Honor Board; my best friends have given me a fabulous present; I feel fine."

Roni shrugged her shoulders. "Just checking." She traced out the design of Terry's striped bedspread with her finger. "Are you studying *already*?" she asked, glancing up. "Classes have barely started."

Terry nodded. "I just got the textbook. It's for comparative anatomy."

Roni raised her eyebrows. "Really? I thought that most pre-meds took that course their senior year. Isn't it supposed to be really tough?"

"Really tough," Terry said. "But I wanted to get it over with. And I guess I sort of want to test myself—you know, find out how well I can do."

"There's absolutely no doubt about it," Roni said, fluffing out her auburn hair with her fingers, "you're a masochist." She stood and stretched, arching her back in a dancer's pose. "So what else are you taking this semester?"

Terry began to tick off the courses on her fingers. "Well, let's see: the second half of organic chemistry, English, and political science. For poli sci, I've got the same professor Sam had last semester, Dr. Lewis."

Restlessly, Roni got up and turned on the stereo.

"Well, all I can say is that we've got your stretcher ready," she said. "That sounds like a killer of a schedule." She put her earphones on and began dancing to the beat, her eyes closed.

"So what are you taking?" Terry asked.

Roni's eyes opened. "What?"

"I said, what are you taking?!" Terry repeated, raising her voice.

Roni held her arms over her head, doing a slow plié. "Poetry," she said lazily, "with the cutest professor at Hawthorne. And modern dance. History. And golf."

"Golf?" Terry asked, startled. "I didn't know you played golf."

"I don't. Not yet." Roni did a split slowly and then bent forward to touch her toe. "But the class was at the right time. I've got a great schedule— nothing before ten o'clock. And I've got the greatest major in the world."

"Oh, yeah? What's that?"

Roni looked up. "Undecided."

Terry shook her head and smiled. That was Roni for you: totally undecided.

The first week of class started off at a gallop, and Terry found herself racing from one classroom to another. Her comparative anatomy class was the hardest to get to: it was on the top floor of the Science Building. Trying to catch her breath, Terry glanced around the classroom after she found a seat in the second row. The students looked older to her, and she guessed that most of them were seniors. They wore the serious, concentrated look that seemed to go with being in the final year of pre-med at Hawthorne. Nobody was going to giggle or pass notes in *this* class.

The girl sitting next to her leaned over. "You'd think we'd be used to climbing those stairs by now, wouldn't you?" she asked with a laugh. "They're killers."

"Yeah," Terry agreed. She pulled out her notebook and glanced up at the blackboard, where the title of the first lecture was already written: *Strategies for Adaptation in Vertebrate Evolution.* Beneath it was an outline of the lecture. "But actually, this is only my second semester," she added. "So I'm still getting used to the altitude on this floor."

"Second semester? Are you kidding? How come you registered for *this* class?" the girl asked, arching her eyebrows in surprise.

Terry laughed a little. "I guess it was a case of temporary insanity," she said.

"I guess so," the girl replied emphatically. She gestured with her head toward the rest of the room. "The reason everyone in here is a senior is because this course has such a bad reputation. Madison is one of the toughest profs. A real terror, especially with unannounced quizzes." She sighed. "But I figure all the pain and agony will be worth it in the end, when I get that acceptance letter to med school."

Terry opened her notebook and put the date at the top of a clean page. She began to copy the title of the lecture. "Yeah," she said softly. "It'll all be worth it in the end."

All week long, Terry couldn't stop thinking about Friday, the day of the Honor Board initiation at Dean Peters's house. She would finally get the chance to wear her new blazer, to let everyone know that she'd actually made Honor Board. At a tough school like Hawthorne, it was something people really respected. But she wasn't just excited—she was a little worried, too. Joining Honor Board was like announcing that you knew you could live up to a higher standard than everybody else. Would people resent her? What if her first semester grades had been a fluke? And Honor Board members were expected to devote time to community projects. Terry had always been kind of shy. Well, it wasn't that she was shy, exactly. She'd always gotten along with other people. It was just that she liked the kind of life she had right now, where she could just go to class, do her work, and get good grades, without people really noticing her or expecting anything special from her. Honor Board would probably change that.

Terry left the library early Friday and hurried back to the suite to change for the reception. She was going to wear her blazer, of course, with a green plaid skirt and a white blouse. Stacy said that Terry's clothes reminded her of the uniforms she'd had to wear at a Swiss boarding school. Terry decided to look through her closet again. She could wear the brown dress she'd worn to the dean's party last semester—it was a little more like a party dress. But the green blazer wouldn't go with it very well. Better to wear her old, reliable plaid skirt. If it was good enough for the mannequin in the window of Nei-man's, it was good enough for her.

Humming, she stripped off her clothes and headed for the shower. Just as she turned on the water, Roni opened the bathroom door and stuck her head inside.

"Hey Terry—that outfit you've got laid out on the bed. Is that what you're planning to wear tonight, to the Honor Board initiation?"

"Sure is," Terry said, searching for the soap. "Why?"

"Oh, no reason," Roni said nonchalantly, shutting the door.

When Terry got out of the shower, pulled on her robe, and went back to her bedroom to get dressed, she discovered why Roni had asked. The blouse and skirt she had laid out were gone, and in their place was Stacy's green-and-gold print dress, Roni's tan suede pumps, and a gold necklace that belonged to Sam.

"Okay you guys, what's going on? Where are my clothes?"

Loud giggles came from behind the door to the living room, and Terry yanked it open.

"What did you do with my clothes?" she demanded.

"What do you mean, what did we do with them?" asked Stacy.

"They're all laid out for you," Sam said.

"But I was going to wear—"

"We know what you were *going* to wear, Terry," Stacy said pointedly. "You were going to wear your schoolgirl uniform. Well, we had a better idea. So we confiscated it."

"Yes, we're thinking of putting that skirt in the incinerator," Roni said.

"And we've got plans for your hair, too." She pulled the curling iron out from behind her back with a flourish. "Is the patient ready?"

"Oh no, you don't," Terry said, backing up. "I don't have time to get my hair curled. And anyway, I don't really like curls. They're not my style. I'd feel funny."

"We don't care how you *feel*." Stacy grinned. "It's how you *look* that we care about. And anyway, you don't have a style—not yet, anyway. Come on, relax. Sit down and let us do your hair. Pretend you're at a beauty salon. Read a magazine. File your nails. Call me Laverne."

"There," Roni said half an hour later as she finished spraying Terry's curls. "How do you like it?"

Terry stared at herself in the mirror. Her eyes widened in surprise. "I don't know. Who is it?" She was wearing a touch of eye-shadow, pink blusher, and lipstick—all of which seemed to give her face definition. Her cheekbones looked higher, her eyes deeper. And her hair looked better than it had in her entire life. It actually *did* something for once, bouncing lightly on her shoulders in a mass of fluffy brown curls.

"Presenting Terry Conklin," Sam announced, with a deep bow. "The *new* Terry. The girl the world has been waiting for."

"Infinitely prettier than the *old* Terry," Stacy said smugly.

"And *much* sexier," Roni added.

Terry looked into the mirror again. She didn't know about the sexy part, but she had to agree with Stacy. She certainly looked much prettier. Just because she was going to an Honor Board party didn't mean she had to look like a grind.

The sidewalk was crowded with kids on their way to dinner at the Commons dining hall.

Terry was hurrying along toward Dean Peters's house trying to keep from spraining her ankle in Roni's high heels, when she heard somebody calling her name.

"Terry? Terry Conklin, is that you?"

She turned around. Brian Benson was standing on the sidewalk behind her, looking at her curiously. He had a skateboard and a few notebooks under his arm.

"Of course it's me," she said, with a self-conscious laugh. "Who'd you think it was?"

"I don't know," he said, grinning. "You certainly look different." He came toward her, pretending to peer at her near-sightedly through his sunglasses.

"That's because I'm not carrying a load of text-books and I don't have a pencil behind my ear," Terry retorted, laughing. "And my head's not bent over a microscope, either."

"No," Brian said. "I think it's because you've got your hair curled." He frowned in a puzzled way. "Hey, isn't that an Honor Board blazer? What are you wearing *that* for? I think that Halloween was *last* semester, Terry."

"Very funny," Terry said, straightening her shoulders. "But I *am* an Honor Board member. Or rather," she glanced at her watch, "I will be in the next hour. I'm on my way to the initiation now, over at Dean Peters's house."

She paused with a smile, waiting for Brian's congratulations. He'd studied with her last semester and had to know just how much Honor Board meant to her.

Brian reached out one hand and gently fingered her jacket sleeve. "Hey, wow," he said, as if he were awe-struck. "Mind if I touch you? Maybe some of whatever you've got going for you will rub off on me." He grinned teasingly, but there was pride in his eyes, and when he spoke again, his voice was soft and Terry could tell he was being sincere.

"That's really great, Terry. It couldn't happen to a nicer girl."

Chapter 3

"Hey, Terry, congratulations," a boy said, suddenly appearing at Terry's elbow. He leaned closer, peering at the name tag pinned on her blazer. "I mean, it *is* Terry Conklin, isn't it?"

Startled, Terry whirled around, almost spilling the cup of fruit punch she held in her hand. The boy's dark hair and brown eyes were familiar — where had she seen him before?

"Rob Goodman. From the theater department." The boy smiled at her. "You know, you really look different. I thought I recognized you when you went up to get your pin from Dean Peters, but I wasn't sure."

"Oh, *now* I remember," Terry said, suddenly recognizing the boy. "You're the director's assistant, right?" The semester before, her work-study assign-

27

ment had been in theater; she'd helped with the costumes. Rob was the one with the clipboard permanently attached to his arm, who made sure that everybody was doing what he or she was supposed to do. Terry admired his ability to manage a dozen things at once without losing track.

"So what do you think of the Honor Board initiation?" Rob asked, taking a bite of his tiny sandwich.

Terry put her cup down on the table beside her. "It's nice, I guess." She looked around. Everybody was standing in tiny little groups, having polite conversations and making sure they were on their very best behavior. "It's a little more formal than I expected, though."

Rob nodded. "I suppose you mean the part where you had to hold up the candle and recite the honor pledge and the Hawthorne creed." He laughed. "Well, I guess it goes with the territory."

Terry laughed too. "Yeah. Well, I guess it's worth it. And I only have to do it once—I hope."

Rob finished his sandwich and together they moved away from the refreshment table. "Are you going to be back in the theater department this semester?"

Terry shrugged. "I won't know until Monday, when I get my work-study assignment. But I'd like to—it was fun. The only problem is, working there every afternoon means that I wind up spending most of my evenings in the library or the lab."

"Yeah, I guess so," Rob said. As he spoke, Terry noticed that his eyes weren't exactly brown—they were brown with little gold flecks, and his hair had blond highlights in it from the sun. He was pretty cute, come to think of it. "So I guess I ought to say double congratulations, Miss Conklin. It's hard enough to make Honor Board—but making it in your freshman year when you're also holding down a work-study job is a pretty big achievement. In my book, anyway. What's your major?"

"Bio-chem," she said. "I'm pre-med."

"Wow!" Rob whistled and raised his eyebrows. "*Triple* congratulations. That's a big load you're carrying. I don't think I could carry a load like that. You must be pretty well organized."

"Not really," Terry said, hoping he wouldn't notice how red her cheeks were. She laughed a little. "I make a lot of lists, mostly."

"You know, I'm curious about your major," Rob said, leaning toward her. "What kind of medicine are you planning on getting into? Eventually, I mean."

Terry hesitated. "I'm not exactly sure just yet," she said. "I've been thinking of—"

"Oh, *here* you are," an extremely pretty blond girl said, putting a proprietary hand on Rob's arm. "I've been looking all over for you. We're going with Suzie and Rich for a pizza."

"Okay," Rob said, shrugging his shoulders. He turned back to Terry. "I'd like to hear more about that," he said. "I hope you'll be coming back to theater this semester."

"So do I," Terry said. "See you later."

Watching the two of them walk out the door, Terry felt a little disappointed. Of course, any boy as nice-looking as Rob Goodman was bound to have a girlfriend. She should have known that. But she couldn't help wishing that she'd gotten to finish her sentence anyway.

Terry woke with a start. "Oh no, I'm late for organic!" she cried, throwing her covers off and jumping up in bed.

"Terry, please. It's the telephone, not your alarm. I'll get it," Roni said, dragging herself out of bed to the door.

Terry couldn't believe it: it was the middle of the night. Who would call then? Only somebody crazy —like one of Roni's wild friends—or maybe it was a family emergency.

Roni came back into the room. "It's for you."

"For me?" Terry asked. "Who is it?"

"I don't know," Roni said, getting back in bed. "I didn't ask and he didn't say." She climbed under her blanket. "But would you please tell whoever it is," she asked, pulling the pillow over her head, "that six A.M. is a little early to call?"

Terry pulled on her robe and went into the living room, closing the bedroom door behind her. Who would be calling her at six in the morning? Please, she thought, please don't let it be an accident or something seriously wrong at home. She sat down on the edge of the sofa and picked up the telephone. "Hello?"

"Hey, Terry. How are you doing? How do you feel about meeting for breakfast? Say, in half an hour?"

"Brian? Brian Benson, is that you?"

"Yeah, it's me." He paused for a minute. "Well, how about it? I'd really like to see you." He cleared his throat. "I mean, we haven't even talked about our study schedules yet."

Terry shivered. The heat didn't come up in Rogers until nearly seven, and the room was cold. "Yeah, sure," she said, rubbing her eyes sleepily. "We should get together. But how about if we make it lunch instead? I've got to see my adviser this morning about my work-study assignment."

"No," Brian said urgently. "I mean, I'd like to do it sooner, if you can. Like this morning. It's kind of important, don't you think. I mean, we're a team. In the lab, anyway."

"But it's barely 6 A.M.," Terry objected. She looked out the French doors that opened onto the balcony of their suite. The sky to the east was starting to gray, but she could see the streetlights still glittering around Hawthorne Lake, just below their balcony. "Brian, the sun isn't even up yet."

Brian chuckled. "That's because it's raining."

"No, that's because it's too early, for Pete's sake. I need eight hours of sleep, and I should think you do, too."

"So what?" Brian replied. "I have to talk to you. So how about it? Half an hour?"

"No, more like an hour, if anything," Terry countered. "The dining hall doesn't open until seven." She frowned, beginning to be a little concerned. "What's up, Brian? Is everything okay? Is something wrong?"

Brian hesitated. "No, not really," he said finally,

"I just want to talk to you, that's all. See you in an hour."

"Okay. Bye," Terry said, hanging up the phone with one hand and rubbing her sleepy eyes with the other.

"Who was that?" Stacy asked, coming out of her bedroom. She pulled her sweatshirt on over her running shorts.

"It was Brian. Sam, are you crazy, too? Are you going running in the rain at six A.M.? What's *happening* to the Hawthorne student body?"

"It's only drizzling, Terry. Calm down. What did Brian want?"

"I don't know," Terry replied, standing up and stretching. "But we're going to have breakfast in an hour." She looked at Stacy critically. "You're going to get your hair wet if you don't wear something over it."

"Terry," Stacy sighed, straightening up. "You're a wonderful girl and I love you, but when did you get your *mother's* license?"

The dining hall was nearly deserted when Terry arrived at five minutes after seven. She shook the water off her umbrella and pulled off her poncho.

"There you are," Brian said. He ran his hand nervously through his brown hair, which was already pretty ruffled up from the rain. "I was beginning to wonder if maybe you weren't coming after all."

"Brian, I'm only five minutes late," Terry said, folding up her umbrella. "I practically had to swim across the bridge. It's coming down buckets out there. You know I wouldn't stand you up."

Brian sighed. "I know. Sorry, I don't know what's gotten into me lately." He took her umbrella and nodded toward a table. "I got you some cereal. With raisins, the way you like it."

Terry smiled and followed him. Sometimes Brian could be a little demanding, but he was basically a nice, extremely thoughtful guy. And he was so serious about doing well in school that you had to admire his dedication. "Is there orange juice too, sir?" Terry asked.

"Tomato. Or is that 'tomah-to'? Who cares. The orange juice has an out-of-order sign on it."

"Oh, okay. Thanks." Terry sat down and looked around at the empty cafeteria. "Do you realize that we are the *only* people having breakfast this early? The orange juice machine is probably on strike." She looked searchingly at Brian. "So what's the problem?"

Brian picked up his fork. "Oh, no problem," he said, with a casual grin. "I just thought maybe it would be a good idea to compare our schedules and see when we could get together to study."

Terry stared at him. She was dying to ask why they couldn't have waited until lunch, but she thought better of it. "Well, okay." She reached down and picked up her notebook. "Let me give you my schedule. What does yours look like? I know we're not in any of the same sections, but I bet we're taking some of the same courses. It'll be good to have a study partner. I think it worked out really well last semester. Don't you?"

"Well, I . . ." Brian's grin faded and he rubbed his

forehead nervously as he looked down at Terry's schedule. "I'm taking the same political science course you are," he said. "But to tell the truth, Terry, I've got to take a couple pre-med courses over again."

Terry blinked. "You're kidding!"

Brian swallowed and looked at Terry. "I wish I were. But the truth is, I failed a few classes."

Terry's mouth fell open. "Oh, Brian, I can't believe that! That's awful." She thought of all the hours he had put into studying, and all for nothing.

Brian sighed and began to eat his eggs. "Yeah, well, it's not so bad," he said. He managed a slight grin. "At least I've already done the reading. And I've been through the lab manuals already."

"But we did some mock finals together and you did okay. What happened?"

Brian shrugged carelessly. "I don't know. I guess I just don't do very well on the real thing. When I gt into my finals, I just forgot everything I ever knew." He pushed his plate away. "So they put me on sco pro."

"Sco pro?" Terry stared at him. "I'm sorry to sound so dumb, but what does *that* mean?"

His laugh had a harsh edge to it. "*Sch*olastic *pro*bation, that's what it means. It means I have to practically ace everything this semester in order to get my GPA high enough to stay in school."

"Ow," Terry breathed. "That's a lot of pressure."

"You know it," Brian said. He picked up a paper napkin and began to pleat it. "Actually," he said, not quite meeting her eyes, "I've been thinking about maybe just dropping out of the program." He kept looking down at his fingers, playing with the napkin. "Or maybe dropping out of school for a couple of semesters. You know, until I get my act together. I sort of wanted to know what you . . . well, what you thought about it."

"Drop out?" Terry asked, staring at him aghast. "Brian Benson, you can't do that! If you dropped out, it would show up on your record and then you'd *never* get accepted to a good medical school."

Brian sighed and began to rip the napkin in little pieces. "Yeah," he said. "That's what my father says, too. 'You can't do that, Brian,'" he mimicked, in a deep voice. "'You have to stay in school and get good grades so you can be a great doctor someday.'" He shook his head. "Unfortunately, the doctors in my family go all the way back to the Civil War— maybe all the way back to the Revolution, for all I know. In my family, being a doctor is a sacred trust." He laughed, and the laugh grated against Terry's ears. "Or a curse, depending on how you look at it."

Terry shook her head, thinking about her brother and how he had felt about being a doctor. Medicine had been something sacred to him, too.

"A curse?" she asked indignantly. "Look, maybe it's tough going, sometimes, and maybe the hours are long and the work is hard. But your father's right: you've got to hang in there, Brian. It'll get better. And I'll help," she added. "At least, as much as I can."

"You will?" Brian asked eagerly. He leaned forward and put his hand over hers. "Listen, Terry, if you'll help me this semester, I *know* I'll do better. I may not get an A in everything, but I'll do well enough to stay in school. And if I can just get through this horrible semester, then I can go to summer school and take something easy to pull up my GPA some more."

"I know you will, Brian," Terry said sympathetically. "You'll see—it'll get better." She glanced at her watch. "Gosh, it's late," she said, pulling back her hand and gulping down the last of her tomato juice. "I've got to run. I have an appointment with my adviser before my first class."

Brian stood up. "Listen, Terry, thanks for meeting me this morning. And I'm glad you're going to help me out. Do you think you could meet me at five o'clock, at the library. Just for a few minutes? I'm going to try to get copies of my finals and see where I screwed up."

Terry nodded. "Yeah, that sounds like a good plan." She looked down at the table. Brian had barely touched his breakfast, and he usually ate everything in sight, including anything she left on *her* plate. "Aren't you going to finish your eggs?" she asked. "They're getting cold."

"Yes, ma'am. Whatever you say," Brian said. "If it'll help me get better grades, I'll try anything."

"Don't forget your Wheaties!" Terry called over her shoulder as she walked past the cash register.

Chapter 4

"Great! You got reassigned to the theater for another semester," Rob Goodman said, walking into the backstage supply room.

Terry looked up from the inventory list she was checking against a trunkful of costume accessories. "Yes." She smiled, pleased. "My work-study adviser said somebody here requested me back."

Rob grinned. "Yeah, well, the director and I had a talk about it and we decided we liked the way you worked. Unfortunately, a lot of the other work-study students we get here aren't really interested in *working*. They want this assignment because they think there's something glamorous about the theater. Then they get caught up in the illusion of it and forget that there's a lot of work involved with *creating* that illusion."

Terry picked up a peach-colored straw hat with a veil and a huge mass of flowers piled on the crown. "Well," she said, examining the hat for signs of damage, "it's not the illusion by itself that interests me." Absently, she put the hat on her head and began to search the list, looking for the item number. She found it and checked it off.

Rob sat down on another trunk. "You're not into fantasy and illusion?"

Terry picked up another, smaller hat. "A little fantasy once in a while doesn't hurt," she said, "as long as you don't get lost in it."

"And what about illusions? Don't you have any?"

Terry shook her head. "I'm a practical person. I like knowing exactly how things are." She put the hat back into the trunk.

"Then what is it that you like about the theater? Are you interested in acting?"

"No," Terry said firmly. "Definitely not. I would never want to be onstage, with everyone watching me." She thought for a minute. "I guess what I like is being around and seeing how everything goes together to *create* the illusion. I've always liked getting a behind-the-scenes look."

"Oh, so you've done theater before you came to Hawthorne, then," Rob replied.

Terry picked up a lacy shawl and inspected it. "A little—not as much as I wanted, because I had a job. But I worked on a stage crew one semester. I like the backstage stuff—watching the stage designers build the sets, and the costume and makeup people dress up the characters, and the actors create the characters. It always seems like a magician's trick to me. We begin with a bare stage and in just a few weeks, abracadabra, we've got a complete play." She threw the shawl over her shoulder and bent to look into the trunk. She hadn't meant to run on about herself like that, but he had seemed interested.

Rob regarded her thoughtfully. "You know, you look terrific in that hat," he said. "You've got exactly the right shoulders and neck."

Terry's head jerked up and the hat fell off. "Oh," she said. She could feel herself blushing.

Rob picked up the hat and turned it in his hands. "We're doing *My Fair Lady* this semester," he said thoughtfully. "You know, Eliza Doolittle doesn't have any illusions, either."

Terry nodded. "I *like* Eliza," she said. "She's got a lot of courage, going up against everybody's expectations and still managing to—"

The door opened. "Hey, Rob, the director wants you out front," a boy said. "Pronto."

Rob stood up and grinned. "That's the second time that's happened to you," he said. "Why don't we finish this conversation later, when there aren't so many interruptions. How about a Coke at the Eatery—around five, maybe?"

For a minute, Terry stared at him, not believing what she'd just heard. Rob Goodman was asking *her* for a date? Just her luck—it was the one day she already had plans.

"I'm sorry," she said. "I wish I could, but I've got to meet somebody at the library at five."

"Your boyfriend?" His question was casual, but not innocent. Terry's heart beat faster.

"No," she said. "Just a friend. Somebody I'm tutoring." She cleared her throat. "I could . . . I could meet you a little later," she ventured.

"Rats," he said. "I've got something to do later." Instantly Terry thought of the pretty blond girl she'd seen with Rob at the Honor Board initiation. "But maybe tomorrow."

The door opened again. "Hey, Rob," the boy said, "Eric says to tell you if you don't come now, he'll come after you. With his lasso."

"Sorry," Rob said hastily. He put the hat on Terry's head, patted her on the shoulder, and then disappeared with a grin.

For a few seconds Terry sat without moving. Then, still wearing the hat and with the shawl over her shoulder, she got up and stood in front of the mirror that hung beside the door and stared at herself. She was still blushing.

It had drizzled off and on all afternoon, but the rain finally stopped when Terry got to the library. She made her way to the back of the second-floor study area, where she and Brian had always worked last semester. He was already there at a table by the window, his head bent over a book.

"Hi, Brian," Terry said, sitting down across the table from him. "How's it going?"

"Hi," he said. "Let me make some room for you." He pushed the stack of books to one side. "Hey, I'm really glad we're doing this, Terry. I mean, I don't think I need a lot of help, but since you and I worked together so well last semester, it seems like a good idea. Don't you think so?"

Terry nodded, smiling a little at Brian's enthusiasm. "You're right, it is a good idea. Were you able to get copies of your finals from last semester?"

"No," Brian said, in a disgruntled tone. "Perkins said it was his policy never to give out old finals, and Matthews asked me if I was gong to study them for this semester or whether I planned to sell them to the highest bidder in the dorm." He laughed a little. "So I guess we're gong to have to do without them."

Terry sighed. "Well, I see their point. I'm sure there's a good market for used finals." She looked at Brian's biology book, lying open on the table in front of him. "Do you want to work on biology first? How about if I ask you some questions about the first chapter?"

Brian pushed the book toward her and stretched. "Well, if you want to know the truth, I'm ready for a break," he said with a yawn. "I've been reading this stuff for a couple of hours and I'm really sick of it. It's so boring sometimes. I guess I'm not feeling very motivated." He turned to Terry with a grin. "So how'd *your* day go?"

"You mean, since you woke me up at six A.M. and dragged me out into the rain?" Terry asked teasingly. "Well, I guess it wasn't so bad." She thought of her conversation with Rob Goodman. "Actually, it was a pretty good day, all in all. A couple of really nice things happened."

"Oh, yeah?" Brian asked. He leaned forward

with his elbows on his knees and peered at her curiously. "Like what kind of really nice things?"

"Well, I got my work-study assignment," Terry said, "and I'm working in the theater department again this semester. In fact, they liked my work so much last semester that they asked me to come back." She leaned back in her chair and looked out the window at the lake, which was begining to fade into the gray twilight. A boy and a girl were walking on the bridge, hand in hand. "It's nice to know that somebody appreciates you."

"Yeah, that's great," Brian said with a sigh. "So what else? I mean, you said a *couple* of nice things happened."

"Oh. Well, I don't know," Terry said, feeling a little funny. The other nice thing was her conversation with Rob, but she didn't really want to tell Brian about it. "Um, I just talked to somebody who's kind of nice, that's all."

Brian grinned and sat back, folding his arms. He looked pleased. "Yeah? Well, I enjoyed talking to you this morning a lot, too. I'm glad we decided to get together this evening."

Terry cleared her throat nervously. She hadn't meant *him*, but there was no good way to let him know that she'd been talking about Rob without hurting his feelings. She hoped Brian wasn't getting the wrong idea about them.

"You know, I didn't really realize how much I appreciated your friendship until I was home for Christmas break. If it hadn't been for you, Terry, being in the pre-med program would've been a real drag. Trying to keep up with classes and everything, I mean."

Terry nodded. Having a friend in the pre-med program, somebody to study with and talk to, really did make a difference.

Brian grinned. "Hey, remember Milt, from biology class last semester? Well, he and Sara are going out now. I saw them together the other day."

"Is that right?" Terry reached for the biology book. "Maybe we'd better get started, Brian. It's getting kind of late."

"Yeah, sure. Well, anyway, he was telling me how neat it is to have a girlfriend in the program — somebody who understands all the pressures. They really support each other, he said."

Terry shrugged, looking through the book. "Yeah, in some ways, I guess it would be kind of nice," she said. "But it might also be a distraction. I mean, the program doesn't leave you a lot of time to pay attention to a relationship." She looked up at him. "How much has Perkins covered in lecture so far? Have you got your class notes handy?"

Brian sighed and opened the green bookbag on the table. "Yeah, they're in here somewhere, I guess." He pulled out an untidy stack of papers and notebooks and began to sort through them. "Biology's in a blue notebook — the same one I was using last semester."

"Is this it?" Terry pulled a notebook out of the

stack. A handful of last semester's lab quizzes fell out of the back.

Brian grabbed it. "Yeah, this is it, all right." He laughed a little guiltily as he picked up the quizzes and stuffed them back into the notebook. "I guess I haven't organized this junk very well, have I?"

Terry looked at him. "You know, Brian," she said thoughtfully, "it might help if you *did* organize this stuff. I mean, it's not *junk*—it's your notes. I know they're pretty good because I've seen them. And since you're repeating the course, last semester's lecture notes and quizzes are a real gold mine. With all this to study from, you shouldn't have any trouble at all. It's not as bad as it looks."

Brian looked at her. "Yeah, you're right. When I get time, I'll put it all in chronological order and really dig into it. In the meantime . . ." he sighed. "In the meantime—I mean, tomorrow, there's a lecture quiz. And I've *got* to do well on it."

"Okay." Terry pulled the book toward her and flipped backward a couple of pages from the place where Brian had been reading. "Let's start with something from the first chapter. Something like cell structure—that's pretty basic stuff." She ran her finger down the page. "So why don't you tell me about mitochondria? How do they work?"

Brian scratched his head, looking puzzled. "Is that in the first chapter?"

"I'm afraid so," Terry said. "We studied it last semester, remember?" She paused, waiting for him.

"Here's a hint: The mitochondria have to do with cell respiration. Why don't you take it from there?"

"Uh, yeah, sure," Brian said, shifting in his chair. "Cell respiration." There was a pause. "Well, then, let me see." Brian didn't say anything for a minute. Then he leaned forward and looked Terry in the eye pleadingly. "Maybe you could read me the paragraph just before the one you took the question from, to sort of get me started."

"Well, okay," Terry said reluctantly. "Here goes." She read the paragraph.

"Oh, of course. Now I remember. Mitochondria. Well, it's like this." He stumbled awkwardly through an answer. "How's that?"

Terry nodded, but gave him a disappointed look. "Well, most of your answer is okay," she said. "But you've left out a couple of important parts of the process." She picked up a yellow highlighter and handed it to him. "Here. Maybe it will help if you underline the functions."

"I can't believe I messed up that way," Brian muttered when they'd finished going through the paragraph. "I mean, it's so simple, and I *know* the answer." He thumped his fist on the table. "I just get too tense, that's all, Terry. When I've got to come up with an answer for a test, I just can't think straight."

"That's okay, Brian," Terry said, with as comforting a tone as she could manage. "Don't let it get to you. Let's do some more of this. It'll get easier as we go along."

But forty-five minutes later, it still hadn't gotten

any easier. Almost all Brian's answers had been like the first one, disorganized and incomplete.

Terry closed the book. "Listen, Brian," she said with a frustrated sigh, "I think that's about all we ought to do this evening. I've got to get started on that paper for poli sci. Maybe it would be a good idea if you worked on something else for a while, and then came back to this stuff in the morning, just before your quiz."

Brian shook his head. "I wish you hadn't mentioned the poli sci paper. I've got to come up with a topic, quick." He looked up, brightening. "Hey, if you're going to work on your paper, why don't you do it here? Then maybe we can go out for a Coke or something after we're finished."

"Sorry, but I've got some books and stuff I need to look at back at the dorm," Terry said, pushing her chair back. She collected her gear. "I hope you get along okay with your studying."

"Well, I really feel a lot better about it now," Brian said, trying to be cheerful. He grinned broadly at Terry. "You're an inspiration, you know. How about getting together tomorrow night? If it's not too much trouble."

Terry didn't know what to say. She didn't want to disappoint Brian, but what if Rob asked her out again? If she said no again, he might give up. "Well, I . . ." She hesitated. "Actually, I might have something else I need to do."

"How about lunch, then?" Brian asked. "By that time, this stupid quiz will be over and I can start thinking about my poli sci paper. Maybe you can tell me what you're doing with your paper, and that'll give me some ideas of my own."

"Well, okay," Terry agreed slowly. She liked Brian, but she didn't want to spend all her free time with him. Especially not now that she had a rain check with Rob Goodman. Second semester was looking better and better.

Chapter 5

"You just missed him," Stacy said. "He called about five minutes ago." She was lying on her stomach in the living room, sketching, when Terry walked in the door.

Terry hung up her poncho in the closet. "Who called?" she asked, holding her breath.

Stacy held up the charcoal sketch of the large pottery pitcher she'd just drawn. "What do you think of this? It's going to be my next project at the pottery studio."

Terry went to the small refrigerator in the corner of the living room and took out a carton of milk. "Stacy, who just called?"

"Don't you think it looks sort of Etruscan?" Stacy sat up and crossed her legs, studying her sketch. "I like the way the handle turns in."

Terry flopped down on the sofa with her glass of milk. "Stacy, will you please stop playing games? I don't have all day. It's a lovely pitcher. Now who called five minutes ago?"

Stacy grinned. "I think he said his name was Rob."

"Rob?" Terry squealed. "You mean, Rob *Goodman* called? He actually did?"

"Watch out," Stacy cautioned, "you're spilling your milk. Yeah, this Rob person has a nice voice. He also wanted to know what time you'd be home. I told him you usually got home about—" The phone rang. "—about now." Stacy smiled. "That's probably him. Aren't you going to answer it?"

Terry stared at the phone for a minute. On the third ring, she picked it up and put her milk down, her hand shaking.

"Hi, Terry? This is Rob. How are you?"

"Uh, hi," she said. "I just got home." She winced —what a dumb thing to say. He knew she'd just gotten home.

"Listen, my meeting was canceled," Rob said, "and I was hoping you'd have time to walk over to Grove Street and get some ice cream at Mickey's."

Terry thought of her poli sci paper and all the reading she had to do. It was only the first week of class, but already her professors were piling on the assignments. But she really wanted to go out with Rob, and besides, she wouldn't let herself fall behind. It was only one night. "Well . . ."

"We won't stay late," Rob promised. "Just long

enough to get personally acquainted with a couple of hot fudge sundaes with nuts and whipped cream."

"It sounds very tempting," Terry said, beginning to smile.

"How about if I call ahead?" Rob asked. "The sundaes will be ready when we get there—no lines, no waiting. We'll get a table for the four of us."

Terry giggled.

"I see here in the student directory that you live in Rogers," Rob said. "I live in Merrill. I'll be over in five minutes."

"Make it ten, okay?" Terry asked and put down the phone. "Quick, Stacy! Do you know where Roni keeps her curling iron?"

"Don't tell me our resident grind is forsaking studying for a date!" cried Stacy in mock surprise. "What's the world coming to?"

Rob and Terry walked slowly around the lake toward Grove Street. The rain was over but there were still a few clouds in the sky, and the moon was casting shadows among the pine trees that bordered the lake. It was getting cooler, and Terry had put on her green jacket and her matching beret.

"So this is your first year at Hawthorne," Rob said, as they walked along.

"Yes. I went to high school in Philadelphia." Terry pushed her hands deep into her pockets. Rob's sleeve accidentally brushed against hers. "How about you?"

"I've been here two years. I'm officially a junior, though. I spent my freshman year at Tulane."

"Isn't that in New Orleans?" Terry asked.

"Right. But I didn't like New Orleans very much," Rob replied. "I mean, I liked being able to hear good jazz in the French Quarter whenever I wanted to. But I've lived in cities all my life, and I decided I wanted to be in a small town for a change. Plus, Hawthorne has a reputation for having a good theater program, so that was another factor." At the corner of the campus, the path branched off toward Grove Street. "What about you? Why are *you* here? Hawthorne Springs is a long way from Philadelphia."

"It sure is," Terry said, then stopped to think about what she should say next. A lot of guys at Hawthorne seemed to be instantly turned off when they found out you were on a scholarship. Maybe it was wishful thinking, but she figured Rob Goodman wasn't one of those guys.

"Actually, I'm here because Hawthorne offered me a scholarship," she said. "I applied to a couple of other schools with good pre-med programs, but I guess my SATs weren't high enough. They were willing to admit me, but they didn't offer me any financial aid."

"You must have done pretty well in high school, then," Rob said matter-of-factly. "I mean, Hawthorne wouldn't have offered the scholarship if you hadn't had a whole lot going for you."

"Yeah," Terry said, kicking her way through a pile of pine needles, thinking about high school. It seemed so long ago—and at least a million miles away. "I didn't have many extracurricular activities because I worked, and my job took up a lot of after-school time. But I did have good grades, and I had done well on the Advanced Placement tests in chemistry and English. So I guess they figured I was a good risk."

Rob grinned down at her under the next street-light. "Well, they figured right," he said. "Honor Board, first semester. Not bad for starters."

Terry nodded, smiling back. Rob's grin was infectious. "It'll do. But good grades don't come easily to me, the way they do to some people. I have to study pretty hard to get where I want to go. You know, they don't let you into medical school unless you've done a superb job as an undergraduate."

When they got to Grove Street, most of the shops were still open, their windows brightly lit. The street was crowded with Hawthorne students walking, riding bikes, on skateboards—most of them carrying books under their arms or in conspicuous knapsacks. Everybody was trying to relax, thought Terry, but nobody had forgotten what they were in Hawthorne Springs for.

"You know," Terry said, changing the subject, "I love walking along Grove Street. It's so different from where I come from."

"The Philadelphia suburbs, you mean?"

Terry gave a short laugh. "Not exactly," she replied. "I grew up right in the city. Not the wealthy section, either."

"You know," Rob said, taking her arm as they stepped off the curb, "you haven't told me yet what kind of a doctor you're planning to be."

Terry could feel the warmth of Rob's fingers on her arm all the way through her coat. So why am I shivering? she thought. "Well, I'm planning to be a surgeon. That's what my brother had decided to do." She stopped herself. She'd never talked to a stranger before about David. But Rob didn't *feel* like a stranger—he seemed like someone she'd known for years. "But he was killed," she said, finally. "He was hit by a drunk driver."

"Was it very long ago?" Rob asked gently.

"Two years ago," she said, swallowing. It still hurt to talk about him. "I was a junior in high school. David was only four years older than me, but he was already in his second year of med school. He was very bright—he skipped some grades—and he had a lot of drive and ambition. He was . . . well, he was just one of those *perfect* people. Everybody thought so. It was a huge shock when he died." She shook her head. "So unbelievable."

"So that's why you're going to be a surgeon? Because he wanted to be one?"

Terry looked up at him, surprised. "No, that's not it at all," she said defensively. "I love medicine. Being a doctor is the biggest, most important thing I can think of to do with my life."

Rob grinned. "Okay, Terry. I believe you."

Terry was silent for a minute. Then she said, "I suppose a lot of it came from David originally. I mean, I used to read his books and we'd talk about what he was doing. I'm sure he passed on to me the way he felt about his work—he was inspiring. But being a doctor is my own idea—my own dream, not just his."

"Well, that's what counts," Rob said. "Having a dream of your own and sticking to it." He glanced up. The red neon sign in the window said MICKEY'S ICE CREAM. "Hey, we're here," he said. "Hot fudge sundaes, here we come."

"So where did you grow up?" Terry asked after they sat down at a small table in the corner.

"I was born in Atlanta. We still live there. Nothing too exciting. My parents host a television talk show there."

Terry looked at him curiously. "A talk show? Hey, I'd say that's exciting. They must be really interesting people."

"Yeah, they are." Rob laughed. "It's kind of hard to keep up with them sometimes, they've got so many different projects going. Occasionally, they produce some other TV shows in Atlanta, and it looks like they're going to be doing more and more of that. I considered staying in Atlanta to go to school, but none of the schools there would let me put together the kind of program I was interested in."

"What's that?"

"Well, I've got an independent-studies major," he replied. "Basically, it means that I designed my own major. I'm majoring in television management. That's why I'm working for the director in the theater program—learning how shows get produced. I've also arranged to do a summer internship with a TV station in Atlanta, so I can learn the technical end of things. And I'll be taking some summer courses in television at Georgia Tech. When I graduate, it shouldn't be too hard to find a job."

"You know, I kind of envy you," Terry said, with a sigh. When *she* graduated, she'd still have med school and her residency ahead of her. "It sounds as if you have everything planned out. You're all ready for life after college. I'll be in med school, then I'll have to do a residency before I can even think about relaxing a little."

"Yeah, that's true," Rob said, looking at her. "It's the nature of the beast." He put down his spoon. "But don't forget, I'm a junior. I have to be more prepared. Besides, I'm always open for wonderful surprises." There was a glint in his brown eyes that gave Terry goose bumps on her arms.

"Yes, I'm talking about you, Terry Conklin," he said softly, as if he'd read her mind. "Surprised?"

Terry looked down at her empty dish. She didn't know what to say. Her heart was pounding, and her breath was uneven. She didn't know whether it was the sugar in the sundae or Rob Goodman that was making her feel so strange.

"Who," she blurted, after an awkward minute, "was the girl you were with at the initiation?" Terry couldn't believe she'd asked that. She looked intently at her sundae to hide her red face. What an awful, tacky, embarrassing thing to ask! But it had been at the back of her mind all evening and she had to know. It was too late to take it back, anyway.

For a minute, Rob just stared at her. "Isabel?" he asked. "Of course, Isabel." He shook his head, laughing. "Isabel is somebody I dated last semester.

We broke up before Thanksgiving, but every now and then we do something together." He grinned at her. "How about you?"

"Me?"

"Do you have a boyfriend on campus? Or back home? Somebody somewhere you're attached to?"

Terry licked her spoon. Roni would know how to play this—she'd shrug and laugh mysteriously, and the guy would go away thinking he was lucky to get an hour of her time. But Terry didn't know how to do that, and she didn't want to make any more mistakes where Rob was concerned. "No, no attachments," she said.

The moon was shining brightly now, and the path around the lake was flooded with silver light. Terry sneaked a sideways glance at Rob—he looked even more handsome in the moonlight. He was holding her hand lightly, and his touch made her feel like floating. She shivered with delight.

"Cold?" he asked.

"A little," she said. She couldn't tell him that she was shivering because she was happy and nervous at the same time.

"Maybe this will help," he said and put his arm around her shoulders. They walked the rest of the way in silence, a warm, companionable silence that seemed to pull them even closer together than talking did. When they got to Rogers House, Rob's arm tightened around her.

"You really *are* a wonderful surprise, Terry Conklin," he said softly. He turned her toward him and put both hands on her shoulders.

Terry didn't know what to do. She was trembling. Was he going to kiss her? She'd only been kissed once before, her junior year, and it certainly hadn't been a very interesting kiss.

Terry didn't get a chance to find out. The door to Rogers opened at that moment, and Pam Mason, the Resident Adviser for Terry's floor, came out with two of the girls from suite 2D. They stood for a minute on the top step, chatting. Pam looked down at Terry and Rob and waved and smiled and one of the other girls, Janette, called over to them.

"Hey, Terry," she said loudly, "if you've got a few minutes later tonight, maybe we could talk about that political science paper that's due next week. Okay?"

Terry gave a resigned sigh. "Okay!" she called back.

With a glance up the stairs, Rob stepped back and dropped his hands. "I guess I don't really want an audience for our premiere," he said, with a little laugh. He touched her face, very gently. "Good night, Terry. I'll see you tomorrow."

"Good night, Rob." Terry watched him walk away, and then she looked up at the silver moon and pinched herself. It was too good to be true.

"So tell me," Roni commanded, flinging herself across her bed, "who is this mystery date who's special enough to drag you away from your studying on a school night?"

Terry put her book down on her desk, took off

her glasses and stretched. "Well," she said, "his name is Rob Goodman. He's a junior, he's tall—"

"Dark, and handsome, too, the way Stacy tells it," Roni said, bending over to pull off her black suede ankle boots. "In fact, she was quite impressed."

Terry grinned archly. "Stacy's got good taste. Say, Roni, maybe you've seen Rob's parents on television. He says they host a talk show in Atlanta. And they've done some other television productions as well."

Roni sat up straight and stared at her. "What did you say his last name was?"

"Goodman. Rob Goodman." She said it again, half to herself. "Rob Goodman."

"You mean, this guy's parents are *the* Goodmans?"

"Well," Terry said, mystified, "I guess so."

"Wow." There was a note of deep respect in Roni's voice. "*You're* going out with the son of Park and Mollie Goodman? What a trip! Terry, that's great!"

"Oh, really? Why?" Terry asked, interested. She propped her chin on her hands and looked at Roni. "I mean, I happen to like *him*, but what's so great about his parents?"

"Oh, they're just about the most popular TV personalities in Atlanta, that's what," Roni said. "Park Goodman does an early-morning show with a live audience, on controversial subjects like drugs and religion—you know, sort of Phil Donahue stuff. Mollie Goodman does commentary on the news, and they've got this neat show for kids that comes on once a month or so." She pulled her red sweater over her head. "I saw them at a party once. They were terrific, telling jokes, clowning around. Is Rob like that?"

"Well, he's got a nice sense of humor," Terry replied, "but he doesn't clown around much." She thought of the way his face had turned silver in the moonlight, and the way his hands had felt on her shoulders. He would have kissed her if Pam and the others hadn't come along, she was sure of it. "Their premiere," he'd called it. She liked that.

"What about Brian?" Roni asked curiously. "I mean, how does he feel about the competition?"

"Competition?" Terry sat up, surprised. "There's no competition. Brian's just a casual friend, not a boyfriend. We study together, help each other out."

"Oh, yeah?" Roni asked. "How many of your 'casual friends' are in the habit of calling at six in the morning?"

"Oh, that." Terry nodded. "Well, Brian's got this problem right now, and he had to talk to me about it." She picked up her book. "He didn't do very well last semester, and now he's on sco pro."

Roni gave her a sympathetic look. "Is that right? Sco pro, that's bad news. And he's pre-med, too. I'll bet he's really feeling the pressure."

"He is. I think it's really getting to him. We worked together for an hour tonight, and he was having a really tough time." She shook her head with a puzzled frown. "I thought it would be *easy* for him the second time around, but I was wrong. It's going to be harder, because he's failed it once already. He's lost what little confidence he once had."

Roni yawned and stood up. "Well, I hope he gets his act together," she said, stepping out of her suede skirt and leaving it in a heap on the floor. "He's a nice guy."

Terry shook her head. Thinking about Brian's problems was depressing. She'd deal with them tomorrow; right now she wanted to think about her wonderful evening with Rob. "Um, Roni," she said hesitantly. "You know that gray angora sweater of yours—the one with the dolman sleeves?"

Roni looked up. "Sure. You want to borrow it?"

"Could I?" Terry never asked any of the girls if she could borrow their clothes. Oh, sometimes they talked her into it—like for the initiation the other night—and they swapped clothes among themselves all the time. But she'd always been comfortable with her own, even if they weren't the most stylish clothes at Hawthorne. And anyway, she hadn't wanted to take the time to dress up. She'd always told herself that she was in school to learn something, not to be a fashion model.

"Listen, I promise to wash it before I give it back," she said, "and I'll be extra-careful not to spill anything on it."

"Don't worry," Roni said over her shoulder, on her way to the bathroom. "It's last year's sweater, and I hardly ever wear it. If you like it, you can have it."

"Really?" Terry asked. It would go beautifully with the gray-and-black plaid skirt she'd found on sale over the holiday. "Oh, no, I couldn't. I mean, I can't take clothes from—"

Roni turned around. "Why not?" she asked. "My closet's so crowded, I can't fit any new spring clothes into it. Hey, you'd be doing me a favor. Honest."

Stacy came into the bedroom, a stalk of celery in one hand and a can of diet soda in the other. "Hey, Roni," she said casually, "what's this I hear about the dean's desk set?"

"What *about* the dean's desk set?" Roni asked, tossing her head with a little grin.

Stacy looked at her. "Oh, there's some sort of rumor going around that somebody jimmied the window in the dean's office last night and climbed in and stole his desk set. You know, the thing that holds a pen and a calendar. It's an antique, I hear." Stacy turned around and looked at Roni's desk, where a heavy brass desk set shone dully. She picked it up and looked at it critically. "As a matter of fact, the dean's set might have looked something like this one."

"Oh, is that right?" Roni drawled innocently. "Now, isn't that *interesting*?" She turned away and picked up her robe. "I think I'll take a shower. Terry, you don't want the bathroom just now, do you?"

Terry looked at the desk set and frowned, a knot of concern beginning to form in her stomach. "I don't remember seeing this desk set before, Roni. Where did it come from?"

Roni gave a careless shrug, not quite meeting Terry's eyes. "Why, from the dean's office, of course," she said. "Where else?"

Terry stared at her, openmouthed. "But, Roni, that's . . . that's *stealing*! You could get into real trouble for something like this!"

Roni giggled. "Are you kidding? I only did it for fun, that's all. It's not like it was some teacher's grade book, or something really important." She looked form Stacy to Terry. "Hey, why are you guys getting so steamed up about this? It was just a prank, that's all. It was just for fun."

Stacy gave her a long look. "It doesn't sound much like fun to me," she said. "You know, you could give our suite a bad name if you keep up this kind of thing. And I, for one, care about my reputation, even if *you* don't." She turned on her heel and left the room.

"Wow," Roni said, half under her breath. "What's eating her? What's she so upset about? It was just a little prank."

"Roni," Terry said, "don't you think—"

"Listen, Terry, don't worry about a thing." Roni went back over to the closet. "You know, while I'm thinking about it, there's a blouse here that might look nice with your plaid skirt. Maybe you'd like to borrow it, too." She glanced at the desk set. "And I wish you'd forget all about this other thing. It really isn't important."

When Terry went to sleep that night, she dreamed that she and Rob were walking by the lake. It was very dark, and suddenly Rob pulled her to him and kissed her. This time, Pam wasn't around to interrupt.

Chapter 6

Early Saturday morning, Stacy was standing in the living room with a new framed print, eyeing the empty wall over the sofa. Terry had just come out of her bedroom, wearing her flannel robe and slippers.

"Pete gave this to me," Stacy said. "Where do you think I should put it? Over the sofa, maybe? That wall is so blank, it looks terrible. It really needs something."

Terry looked at the print. It was an abstract, mostly reds and blacks, with some orange. "It's a nice present, but I'm afraid it won't go with the sofa very well." The sofa was a green-and-black plaid that looked as if it had been salvaged from somebody's family room—some family with nine kids and a large dog with rather grubby paws, Roni had remarked once.

Stacy sighed. "I'm afraid that *nothing* goes with the sofa very well," she said. "It's absolutely hideous. What happened to that red throw that Roni found for our party last semester? At least it covered up this awful plaid, even if it wasn't the neatest decorating job."

"I think Roni borrowed that from Janette, next door," Terry said. "She might let us borrow it again, if she's not using it."

"Or better yet, we could buy one." Stacy turned around. "In fact, now that we've been here awhile, maybe we ought to think about doing a little decorating. We could use a new rug in front of the sofa, too. Unfortunately, Bandit seems to have eaten the corner of that one."

Bandit was the kitten Stacy had found before Thanksgiving. Pam, the RA on their floor, had evicted him as soon as she'd discovered him—but they'd kept him for a few weeks first. Now he was living over at Pete's house, terrorizing the mice in the Youngs' attic, Stacy said. Sometimes he came over to spend the night in the suite, just for old times' sake.

Terry sighed. "*You* can think about redecorating the suite," she said, pouring herself a cup of coffee from the pot on the hot plate. "*I've* got to think about where under the sun I'm going to find time to run a lab experiment, do a dissection—"

"Do a *dissection*?" Stacy moaned. "Yuk. That sounds gross." She gave a delicate shudder. "I could never be a doctor, never in a million years. The only good thing about being a doctor is the salary, if you ask me."

"And write a paper, and read a few hundred pages—all in one short weekend," Terry finished, taking her coffee with her to the sofa. "Oh, yes, and I also have to be an usher at a piano recital tonight."

Stacy turned to examine the bookcase wall for her new print. "And what about Rob Goodman? Have you left time for him, in the midst of all this frantic pursuit of scholarship?"

Terry leaned back on the sofa and propped her furry slippers on the coffee table. She'd seen Rob twice since their first date for ice cream, both times at the theater. They had both been too busy working to do much more than chat for a few minutes. She'd been convinced that he was going to ask her out for Friday or Saturday, but yesterday she'd found out that he was planning to spend the weekend with his folks. She was disappointed, but at least now she could get some work done. He said he'd call her on Sunday night, after he got back. "If it's not too late," he said, "maybe we can go out for a pizza." She had wanted to say that two A.M. wasn't too late, but she'd restrained herself.

"He's in Atlanta for the weekend," Terry explained, "with his parents." She smiled happily. "We're going to get together for a pizza on Sunday night, if he gets back in time." She sighed. "So all I have to do today is slog my way through that pile of work, and then tomorrow..."

She let her voice trail off and leaned back, closing her eyes and savoring the lovely feeling of warmth and happiness that flooded through her whenever she thought about Rob. So what if they didn't really have a definite date for Sunday night—he wanted to take her out. She hoped he would get back in time. Funny thing, she'd only known him for a week— well, she knew him last semester, but that really didn't count—and they'd only been out together once. But already he was one of the most important people in her life.

There was a knock on the door. Stacy propped the print against a chair and went to open it.

"Hi. Is Terry here?"

Terry sat up and put her coffee mug down on the table with a loud bang. It was Brian.

"Yes, she's here," Stacy was saying, "but I don't think she—"

"Listen," Brian said, "I'm sorry to barge in like this so early on a Saturday morning, but I really have to see her. I mean, it's important."

Terry sighed and stood up. "It's okay, Stacy," she said, and Brian brushed past Stacy into the room. Terry put a hand to the curlers in her hair. "I don't exactly look like Princess Di, but—"

"Listen, I know I should have called before I came over," Brian said. "But I've been working on that experiment that was due yesterday, and I want you to come over to the lab and check it for me before the TA grades it." He stopped, staring at her. "What are those funny-looking things all over your head?"

Terry yanked her robe around her. "Those are curlers," she said indignantly, feeling her face get red. "They're part of an experiment *I'm* doing. And if you don't like the way they look, that's too bad."

"I'm sorry." Brian bowed his head. "I didn't mean

to make you mad. Will you come over with me? Check the experiment, I mean?"

"I don't have time to do it this morning," Terry replied, feeling a little aggravated. "I've got a ton of my own work to do, Brian. A ton. And anyway, the teaching assistant won't be around the lab this weekend. Nobody else will touch it if you leave a note on it. Just leave it set up and I'll stop by and look at it early Monday morning. That'll be soon enough."

Brian's face sagged. "No, it won't," he said. Wearily, he rubbed his hand through his hair. "Listen, Terry, I've been up half the night working on this experiment. The TA promised he'd come in sometime this weekend to grade it for me—maybe this morning. If it's good, he'll forget about the fact that it's late. But if it's not, I'll really be in trouble. You *have* to check it and see if it's okay first." His voice sounded tense and strained. "Please? If I've screwed up, I won't get any credit for it, and I'll have to do it again and—"

Terry held up her hand. "Listen, it's okay, I'll go." Brian looked so tired that she really felt sorry for him. "I've got to go to anatomy lab anyway, so I can stop by for a few minutes." She looked at the clock on the refrigerator. It was only nine o'clock. "I can't get over there for an hour or so, though."

"Listen, that's fine," Brian said quickly. "That's great." He took a step toward the sofa. "How about if I just sort of hang around here while you get ready? I can read or something while you get changed."

"No, don't wait here for me, Brian," Terry said, trying not to let her impatience show. "I've got some other things I have to do before I'm ready to leave. Why don't you just go on back to the lab, and I'll meet you there." She looked at Brian. His face looked sort of gray, and his eyes were a little too bloodshot and bleary. "On second thought, why don't you go back to your room and get some sleep for an hour? You look like you need it."

Brian nodded. "Yeah," he said, giving her a grateful look. "Hey, it's nice of you to think of me. Now that you mention it, I guess I could use a nap."

"Well, then," Terry said in a soothing tone, "how about if I call your room and wake you up before I go over to the lab?"

Brian nodded. "That'd be great. Good. Okay. Gosh, Terry, I appreciate everything you're doing to help. I really do. You're a super friend." He backed toward the door, with a nervous nod at Stacy. "I'll see you over at the lab," he said, and left.

Stacy stared after him. "That was *Brian*?" she asked, after the door had closed. "The same guy you went to the Merrill formal with?" She shook her head with a puzzled look. "Wow, he sure has changed. The guy I remember seemed to laugh once in a while. This guys looks like the messenger of doom."

"Yeah, I know," Terry said with a sigh. She had other things to worry about, but Brian's problem was beginning to seem pretty serious. "To tell the truth, I'm sort of worried about him. He's got problems with his grades, and he can't seem to pull himself together."

Stacy winced. "Grade problems? Yeah, I know something about that. In no time flat, you can dig yourself into a hole so deep you can't even see the sky."

Frowning, Terry refilled her coffee cup and poured some granola into a bowl. "The thing is, now he's on scholastic probation and he's afraid of getting kicked out of school. So he panics even more when he has a test or quiz or anything—and then he does even *worse*."

"So is he going to make it?"

Terry shrugged. "I'm not sure that all the studying he's doing is really helping. I've been working with him an hour a day, and sometimes the stuff just seems to go over his head. But he's pouring everything he's got into it. I've got to give him that much credit—no pun intended."

Stacy frowned at Terry. "He looks like he's pouring himself into an early grave, if you ask me. He looks a little haunted." She began to look through a drawer.

Terry sat back down on the sofa and began to eat her cereal. "He is," she said, "by the ghosts of doctors past."

"The ghosts of what?"

"Everyone in Brian's family has been a doctor. All of the men, anyway. Back to the Civil War and beyond. A lot of doctors seems to come from medical families—it's sort of a common thing. Something about it seems normal."

"But it's not a normal thing to kill yourself with work," Stacy remarked, still looking through the drawer. "Didn't I see a nail in here the other day?"

"Oh, I don't know. I haven't seen it. Maybe he's

overworking himself," Terry replied, "and once he feels better about himself, he'll relax a little. After he gets a good grade or two—like on this experiment today—he'll probably bounce back. He just needs some help, that's all."

"Here it is," Stacy said triumphantly, holding up a nail. "But don't you think that maybe a regular tutor would be better? Someone who's trained to help underachievers? And someone he isn't involved with?" She began to pound the nail into the wall over the sofa, using the heel of her shoe as a hammer.

"But he's not involved with me," Terry objected. "I'm getting involved with somebody else." She colored. "I mean, I *hope* I am."

"Well, you may not be interested in Brian," Stacy observed thoughtfully, "but Brian's definitely interested in you."

Terry put her spoon down. "You bet he is," she said firmly. "He's interested in how much I can help him with his schoolwork. He knows I've done all those lab experiments before and I know how they're supposed to turn out. *That's* what he's interested in."

"Are you sure that's all?" Stacy asked, giving her a searching look.

"That's all," Terry said emphatically. "I'm just a friend. Somebody he turns to for tutoring help. We studied together all last semester. You know that."

"Well, maybe it would be a friendly thing to do to suggest to him that he get somebody else to tutor him."

"I would if I thought it was necessary," Terry muttered. "But I don't."

Stacy picked up the print and hung it on the wall. "So what do you think?" she asked, changing the subject pointedly. "Does this look okay?"

"It looks fine," Terry said. She shook her head. If Stacy wanted to think Brian was interested in her, that was her business. But she was wrong. Sure, maybe they *had* gone to a big formal last semester. And maybe it *did* look like the beginnings of a romance to Stacy and the others. But that wasn't how it was. She'd made it perfectly clear to Brian from the very beginning that their relationship was limited to the classroom and the lab. Nothing had happened to change that.

It was almost six o'clock on Sunday night. Terry let the phone ring three times before she finally picked it up and said hello with studied casualness —as if she hadn't been sitting there *praying* for the call.

"Hi, it's me," Brian said cheerfully.

"Oh," Terry said, taking a deep breath. "How are you?" She cleared her throat. "Um, how did your experiment go? Did the teaching assistant see it yet?"

"I got an A!" Brian exclaimed. "Isn't that great?"

"Hey, that's terrific," Terry said, genuinely pleased. "See—I told you. Everything's going to be okay, if you just hang in there and keep working. You know the material, you really do."

"Yeah, I think you're right," Brian said. "I *know* you're right. I feel a thousand percent better already. Hey, how about celebrating? We could go over to the

PizzaRoo and get a large with everything—except anchovies, of course. Or we could try that new Italian place on Dixon Avenue. I hear they've got great lasagne."

"Oh, that sounds great. But I don't think I can make it, Brian. I wish I could help you celebrate. But I've got an awful lot of studying to do tonight." She wished she had told the truth, that she sort of had plans with Rob. But it was easier to use studying as an excuse—Brian understood studying.

There was no mistaking the disappointment in Brian's voice. "Oh. Well, okay, another time, maybe. Rain check?"

"Rain check," Terry answered automatically. Then she wished she hadn't said that, either. She didn't really want to go out on a date with Brian, especially after talking to Stacy. Stacy was wrong, she was sure, but there was no point in letting Brian get any ideas about the two of them. She'd help him with his work because she was his friend and she wanted him to succeed, but that was as far as it went.

Rob called just as Terry put the phone back on the table. Terry was so surprised, she almost knocked the phone onto the floor.

"Hello," she said, laughing.

"I'm back and I'm starved," Rob announced. "So what's so funny about that? Are you ready for that pizza, or what?"

"I sure am," Terry said fervently. "Studying always makes me hungry."

"Great," Rob said. "How about the PizzaRoo?"

Terry hesitated. What if Brian was there? Maybe they should go someplace else. But why should it matter whether Brian was there or not? She wasn't obligated to him. Besides, Hawthorne Springs was so small that no matter where you went, you always ran into someone you knew. It wasn't as if you could hide, even if you wanted to. That was something they'd all learned first semester, especially Stacy.

"The PizzaRoo is fine," she said. "What time is it now? Six o'clock? Give me fifteen minutes." She began pulling the curlers out of her hair. "I've got to finish an experiment."

It was almost nine when Rob walked Terry back to the front steps of Rogers. "I'd ask you in," she said, "but I've got to study." She clapped her hand over her mouth. "You know, that's gotten to be such a habit that the words just come out automatically. 'I've got to study.'"

Rob sighed. "Me, too. I guess that's our theme song, isn't it? I'll be up until two A.M., doing the homework I should have been doing all weekend. But procrastinating was worth it—especially the last few hours of it."

"It *was* fun," Terry said. "I'm sorry it's over," she added impulsively.

Rob moved closer and put his hand on Terry's shoulder. "I want to kiss you," he said very softly. "I've been wanting to kiss you all evening. And this time, I don't care who's watching. Or whether or not either of us has to study."

"Neither do I," Terry whispered, looking longingly into Rob's brown eyes.

"Good," Rob said, pulling her gently toward him.

With his lips on hers and his arms around her, it wouldn't have mattered to Terry whether all the residents of Rogers House had come out and lined up on the stairs to watch. And if they had, they would have been shocked to see suite 2C's resident bookworm kissing one of the handsomest juniors at Hawthorne.

Chapter 7

Roni looked up from the stack of cassette tapes she was sorting as Terry walked in from her date with Rob. "So, did he kiss you?" she demanded.

"Maybe he did, maybe he didn't," Terry countered with a grin, pulling off her jacket. "How come you guys have to know *everything* that goes on? Aren't I entitled to any privacy?"

"Yeah, Roni," Sam said. She looked up from her crossword puzzle and took another handful of popcorn out of the bowl on the floor, as Terry sat down beside her. "Do we ask you to tell us *your* secrets—like where you go when you don't come home until three or four in the morning?"

Roni shrugged and blushed a little. "Maybe I'd tell you if you asked," she said, with a careless shrug.

She popped a tape into the stereo and rolled over onto her back. "I don't remember your asking."

"Well," Terry said, glad that the attention had shifted from her, "why don't we start with where you were last night?"

"Right," Sam said. "I heard you come in at four-fifteen. Now, Hawthorne Springs rolls up the sidewalks at eleven, and even the Party Barn out on Patterson Road closes its doors at two."

Stacy came out of the bedroom with a towel tied turban-style around her head. "Yeah," she said, "I want to hear this, too. You woke me up when you tripped over the chair."

"Last night . . . last night." Roni made a teepee out of her fingers and looked up at the ceiling as if she were trying to remember. "Oh, yes. Last night. Well, let's see. I went over to my friend Jana's and then we picked up some guys she knows and went out to the Party Barn until they turned out the lights on us, and then we went back to Jana's apartment with a couple of six-packs and listened to music and danced." She grinned at Sam. "So how's that for an exciting night life?"

Sam shook her head and took some more popcorn. "Wild," she said, with mock disapproval. "Truly wild."

Roni turned to Terry. "Okay, I've fessed up— some of it, anyway. Your turn. Did Rob kiss you?"

Terry nodded, then winced when the others clapped and whistled. She could feel herself blushing. It was nice of them to care what happened to her and whether she was happy or not, but she didn't really want to be teased about Rob. "I'm getting out of here before I'm interrogated any more." She got up and started for her bedroom when the phone rang.

Sam picked it up. "It's for you," she told Terry, talking with a mouthful of popcorn. "It's a boy."

Terry took the receiver with a rush of anticipation.

"You know," Stacy told Sam with a grin, "this sudden popularity is definitely having an effect on Terry's personality. Have you noticed?"

"What I've noticed," Sam said, going back to her puzzle, "is that she *looks* different, now that she's doing her hair and wearing a little bit of makeup. Don't you think so?"

"What *I* think," Roni said, getting a diet soda out of the refrigerator, "is that she ought to get her hair permed. She doesn't have time for boys, studying, Honor Board, *and* curling her hair." She looked around. "Who wants something while I'm up?"

"I do," Sam said. "How about a glass of mineral water for me?"

"Hey, you guys," Terry protested, "I can't hear! Would somebody turn down the stereo?" She turned her back on the others. "Excuse me, what did you say?"

"I said that I thought you had to *study* tonight."

Terry gulped. "Brian? Is that you? What's the matter? Why are you—"

"Never mind about me. It's *you* we're talking about. You said you were studying tonight. You were too busy to go out with me and celebrate. But you had plenty of time to go out with somebody else."

"But I—"

"Did you think I wouldn't see you? Or didn't you care? I mean, you *could* have gone someplace else in Hawthorne Springs, you didn't have to go to the PizzaRoo. Or were you doing it on purpose, to rub my nose in it? Listen, Terry, if that's what you had in mind, I'd say it was a pretty lousy thing to do."

Terry took a deep breath, feeling the heavy weight of guilt descend on her shoulders. "No, I wasn't doing it on purpose," she said. "I'm sorry, Brian. I'm really sorry. I mean, I didn't have any *definite* plans, but I guess I should have told you that I was waiting for somebody else to call. And maybe Rob and I should have gone someplace else to eat, but I really didn't think it would matter to you, even if you did see us."

"And then! Then you let him kiss you, right out in front of Rogers, where anybody could walk right by and see what you were doing."

Terry stared at the phone, the anger boiling up inside her. "You followed us back to the dorm?" she asked. Behind her, the room was suddenly silent. "You stood and *watched* us?"

Brian cleared his throat. "Hey, I live in Baxter, don't I?" he said defensively. "I have to walk past Rogers to get home, don't I? Anyway, you guys were putting on quite a show, right out there on the sidewalk. Who could miss it?"

"Listen, Brian," Terry said furiously, clenching the phone so hard her knuckles were turning white, "that's about the most *rotten* thing I've ever heard of.

What gives you the right to stand around and *spy* on people? What I do is none of your business."

"I wasn't spying, damn it!" Brian shouted. "I was just walking by!" He slammed down the phone.

"Ahem," Stacy said, into the silence.

"Hey, Terry," Roni said in alarm, looking up from her stack of cassettes, "what's wrong? What was that all about?"

"It was Brian," Terry said blankly, staring at the phone.

"Brian?" Sam asked. "He was watching you? Why?"

"I don't know," Terry said. She rubbed her mouth with the back of her hand. A few minutes ago, she hadn't cared who saw Rob kiss her. The whole world could have been watching and it wouldn't have destroyed her happiness. Now, the idea of Brian watching her and Rob kissing made her skin crawl. "He . . . he saw Rob and me together, and it . . . it bothered him."

"*Bothered* him!" Stacy exclaimed. "That's the understatement of the century. I could hear him shouting all the way over here."

"It looks," Roni said in a wise voice, "as if we have a serious case of jealousy on our hands."

"Jealousy!" Terry scowled. "Brian doesn't have any right to be jealous! We've never been any more than friends. All I've done is help him with his schoolwork. He's crazy! Absolutely crazy!"

"Since when," Sam inquired, "has jealousy been a rational emotion?"

"And didn't you tell us that he's having trouble

with his studies?" Roni asked. "Being on sco pro is enough to make anybody sweat. Maybe he just can't get it all together right now, and he just happened to blow up at you over something small like this."

"Hhmh," Stacy snorted. "Sounds to me like Brian is getting to be a real bore. *I'd* tell him to take a hike. If we spent all our time indulging boys with crushes, we'd never have time for anything else."

The phone rang. Terry reached for it, but Sam put her hand on Terry's arm.

"Why don't you let somebody else answer it?" she said.

Looking miserable, Terry nodded, and Stacy picked up the phone. "I'm sorry," she said, in an icily polite voice, "but Terry can't come to the phone right now. May I take a message?" There was a silence. "Yes, I'll tell her." She hung up.

"What did he say?" Terry asked.

"He said to tell you he was sorry, he doesn't know what came over him, shouting like that. And he wants to know"—she frowned—"if you'll meet him at six tomorrow night to study. In the library. Honestly, some people are so rude."

"Do you really think that's such a good idea?" Sam asked. "I mean, maybe it would be better for him to get somebody else to tutor him."

Terry bit her lip. "I don't know," she said. "Maybe you're right. Maybe this is getting much too complicated. I mean, I don't want to give him any ideas about us."

"Listen," Roni said emphatically. "From the sound of it, that guy's *already* got ideas." She turned to Sam and Stacy. "Well, look, you guys, if Terry's going to have half-crazed suitors calling on the phone and banging on the door at all hours, don't you think we ought to have some kind of defense plan worked out in advance?" She looked at the clock on the refrigerator. "It's nearly ten. Let's synchronize our watches. I'll take the first watch, if one of you will take the second."

Terry reached for a magazine with lightning speed. Laughing, Roni ducked, and it banged off the wall behind her head.

Brian apologized again when Terry saw him the next night at their usual hourly session in the library.

"I'm sorry," he said. "I guess I shouldn't have called last night. But I was feeling pretty rotten after . . . I . . . Well, I guess I felt let down, even though I didn't have any reason to be. I mean, it wasn't like we had a date or anything."

"Right," Terry said, opening Brian's biology book. "It wasn't like we had a date."

He frowned. "I hope you're not mad at me, Terry. I'm very sorry if I offended you. I hope you'll let me make it up to you."

Terry shook her head. "I'm not mad. I'd just like to forget about last night. But I *am* getting kind of worried about you." She looked at him. "Are you sure you're getting enough sleep?"

"What's enough?" Brian sighed, rubbing his eyes. "I mean, I could sleep all day and it wouldn't change anything. You know, sometimes I really think I ought to drop out of school. If I don't, I'll go crazy. But I

also know that dropping out's no answer. It would
only tick my dad off." His laugh had a jagged edge.
"It would tick him off if I went crazy, too. In our
family, people don't do things like that."

"Look," Terry said, thumbing through the second
chapter, "it's not always going to be this bad. If you
can just hang in there, things will get easier."

"Yeah, I know," Brian said glumly. "You keep
saying that."

"Well, that's because it's true," she insisted. He
nodded at her encouraging smile, and they settled
down to work.

The next week was so crazy that Terry didn't have
time to worry about anyone but herself. Her lab assignments began to pile up, and her list of unfinished
reading seemed to get longer every day. There was
an Honor Board meeting on Tuesday evening, and
on Wednesday night Terry had to usher at the student orchestra concert.

Her work-study job at the theater was getting
more and more hectic, too. She saw Rob there every
day and usually managed to talk to him, if only for a
few minutes. Stage rehearsals for *My Fair Lady*
would be in full swing in another week or so, and the
costume room was crowded with actors getting their
first fittings, people searching for props in the boxes
stacked in the corners, and costume assistants sewing
new items. Terry was assigned to Eliza Doolittle,
who was going to be played by Allison Reynolds, a
senior with several years of acting and singing experi-
ence. Together with the costume designer, they

worked out Eliza's wardrobe, and Terry got busy assembling everything she'd need to dress the character as Eliza was transformed from a Cockney flower girl to a great lady.

Friday afternoon, Rob found her in the storage closet, behind one of the clothes racks, looking for a ragged black skirt for Eliza to wear in Act 1. She'd already found the right hat—a little black straw hat with a crooked red flower—and she was wearing it while she hummed the words from Eliza's first-act song, "Wouldn't It Be Loverly."

"You know," Rob said, "you're hard to find, hiding out back here in the closet."

Terry cocked Eliza's hat forward with a silly look on her face. "All I want," she sang, doing a little two-step, "is a room somewhere, far away from the cold night air . . ."

Rob grinned and held out his hand. "Come on, Eliza. You're being promoted."

"Promoted?" Terry asked, pulling a skirt off the rack and holding it up to the light. "Now really isn't a good time for a promotion. I have to finish getting Eliza's costume together before five."

Rob shook his head and handed her a clipboard. "You're far too valuable to spend your time hiding behind the clothes rack." He looked at his watch. "I figure that with your executive ability, you'll have your first three assignments done by five o'clock."

Terry stared at the clipboard. Her mouth dropped open. "What are you talking about? Executive ability? Assignments?"

"We've just lost our production assistant," Rob

explained. "Eric asked me to find another one. I've just found her."

Terry shook her head in alarm and thrust the clipboard back at him. "Listen, Rob, I really *like* my job backstage. I don't want to be a production assistant. Honest."

Rob put a friendly arm around her shoulders. "I know. If you had it your way, you'd spend your entire life backstage, wouldn't you? With the door closed and a book on your lap." He began to sing in a slightly off-key voice. "All I want is a room somewhere . . ."

Terry had to laugh. "Well, not exactly," she began.

"Does that mean you'll do it?" He handed her the clipboard again. "Eric's getting the entire production staff together at four o'clock, and it's almost that now. Come on."

"Hey, wait a minute," she objected, putting her hands behind her. "I didn't say I'd definitely do it yet."

"Rob, Eric's looking for you," a girl said, coming up behind them. "He says on the double."

"Story of my life," Rob sighed. He reached for Terry's hand and began to pull. "Come on. We haven't got time to argue about it." Turning to the girl, he said, "Go tell the costume designer that her right-hand girl has just been stolen. She'll have to find somebody else."

Eric was a shaggy-haired man with bushy eyebrows and a very impatient manner. He peered over the top of his glasses at Terry when Rob introduced them. "Are you well organized?" he barked. "Got a good mind for details?"

"Well, I, uh . . ." Terry began.

"She's pre-med. Honor Board, too," Rob said reassuringly. "And she's been doing a great job on the costumes—lots of detail there. And she knows the production." He winked at Terry. "She even knows the lyrics."

"Okay," Eric said to Terry. "We'll give you a try. As long as you don't sing. Rob, tell her what needs to be done this afternoon. She'll report to you."

Terry swallowed. "Rob," she whispered, when Eric turned away, "do you really think I can do this?"

"Piece of cake," Rob said serenely. "Just watch. Before you know it, you'll be up to your elbows in work, and loving it."

Following Rob's directions, Terry ran a couple of errands, made a half dozen phone calls, and put together of list of things that had to be done during the rest of the week. When the afternoon was over, she and Rob walked out of the theater into the late-afternoon sunlight, spilling warm and golden across the grass.

"It feels like spring, doesn't it?" Rob said, squinting up into the sun. He took a deep breath. "Smells like spring, too."

Terry sniffed. It *did* smell like spring—like damp earth and new leaves. "This is so hard to believe," she said, turning her face up to the sun. "Back in Philadelphia, they're probably having a snowstorm."

"Fortunately, Georgia isn't Pennsylvania." Rob grinned. "Spring comes early down here. First thing you know, there'll be daffodils all over that hillside over there, and the dogwoods will be blooming." He took her hand. "Hey, how about a walk this afternoon? I know spring isn't officially here yet, but it's Friday, and that ought to count for something."

Terry smiled and nodded happily as Rob squeezed her hand tightly and they started off across the campus. The sun was shining brightly, Hawthorne Lake was glimmering, spring was almost here, and she'd just gotten a job that meant she'd be working with Rob every day. Everything was perfect. What more could she ask for?

"Hey, I've been thinking," Rob said, as they crossed the bridge and headed toward the bluff at the other end of the lake. "I'm going to Atlanta this weekend to help my folks with one of their kids' productions. They're taking a bunch of kids out to an airport to do a location filming. I know it's kind of short notice, but would you like to come along? It should be a lot of fun. And I'd like for them to meet you."

"Meet *me*?" Terry asked incredulously.

"Yeah. Can you imagine?" He looked quickly at her, obviously amused. "Well, I have this strange feeling that you're going to be in my life for a while. I'd like them to get to know you. And vice versa."

He grinned. "What do you say, Ter? Would that be okay?"

"Yeah," Terry said, a feeling of almost unbearable happiness welling up inside her. "That would be okay. In a manner of speaking."

Chapter 8

"Are you sure you've got everything, Rob?"

"Yeah, we're sure, Mom," Rob said, giving his mother an affectionate hug. "I checked." He grinned at Terry. "She asks that about ten times whenever I'm getting ready to leave."

Terry grinned back. The trip to Atlanta had been more fun than she could possibly have imagined, and Mr. and Mrs. Goodman's casual, easygoing manner had made her feel at home from the moment they'd said hello. No wonder Rob seemed so together; with parents like these, how could he miss?

"I *know* you checked, dear. But something always seems to get left behind." She turned and gave Terry a warm hug. "You were a wonderful help this weekend, Terry. I don't know how we would have managed all those kids without you." She gave a rueful little laugh and brushed her hand through her short curly brown hair. "Next time I get the bright idea of shooting a show for six-to-ten-year-olds on a Saturday in the Atlanta airport, I hope somebody stops me. Please promise me you'll at least do that, Rob. Boy, shooting in the studio is a luxury compared to shooting on location."

"Yeah, well, it all worked out, Mollie," Mr. Goodman said, putting his arm around her shoulders.

"That's only because Terry and Rob were here to help. They're the ones who ran all the errands and kept everybody together. And I noticed that Terry was telling stories to some of the younger kids to help keep them quiet while we were shooting." She smiled at Terry. "You're welcome anytime, Terry. I hope we didn't work you too hard."

"Oh, no," Terry protested. "I loved it, every minute of it. Thank you so much for everything."

"Well, we hope you'll come back soon. You're a perfect guest."

"Thanks, I will," Terry promised, with a glance at Rob. She hoped that was okay with *him*.

"Drive safely, now," Mr. Goodman said, as they climbed into Rob's little blue Datsun.

"You see?" Rob said, the minute they backed out of the driveway and started on their way back to Hawthorne. "They loved you. You were a real hit."

Smiling, Terry settled back into the seat. "They're pretty neat, too. Hectic as it was, I really enjoyed the shoot on Saturday. But even more than that, I liked watching your folks work together at the studio yesterday. I find the TV studio even more interesting than the theater. There's so much going on, it's incredible."

"Yeah." Rob glanced over his shoulder as he merged onto the highway. "A lot of my friends think it's a drag to spend the weekend with their parents." He shook his head. "I'm glad I don't feel that way."

Terry was silent. His parents were so different from hers that she felt a little envious. But she didn't say anything except, "Yeah, that's great." She sighed and looked out the window.

"Hey, Ter, I was just thinking. You know that midweek study party the Honor Board is throwing over in the first-floor Merrill lounge on Wednesday? Want to go with me?"

"Sure. Thanks. I'd really like that. Hey, Rob? Maybe we shouldn't exactly *hurry* back." She looked at him, her eyes shining.

"Are you going out with Rob again tonight?" Roni asked curiously, as Terry buttoned her new oversize red cardigan sweater. She was wearing straight-leg jeans and had her hair in a bobbing ponytail.

"Yeah. We're going roller-skating. But first I've got to spend an hour helping Brian with organic, so I'm heading over to the library now." She looked into the mirror and added a little blush to her cheeks. "Listen, if Rob calls, tell him I'll be back at seven-thirty, okay?"

"Okay," Roni said. She put down the rock-music magazine she was reading and glanced at Terry. "You know, I just don't understand why you think you have to spend so much time with Brian. With everything else going on in your life, you're running yourself ragged. And he calls you almost every day. Isn't it getting on your nerves?"

"Well, it's no picnic," Terry admitted, pulling on her sneakers. "But I'm only spending an hour a day with him, and maybe a few minutes on the phone, answering questions. Anyway, everything else is going so well that an hour a day with Brian isn't going to hurt me."

It was true. She was so happy about the way things had been going with Rob for the last couple of weeks that it was easy to temporarily forget her concern for Brian. It was almost the middle of the semester, and next week she'd have to start thinking about midterms. And Brian would have to worry about midterms most of all.

"Is he doing better? How about his crush—is he getting over it?"

Terry paused. "I guess he's improving. His homework scores are decent, but he's still having some trouble with tests." She stood up and reached for the stack of library books she had to return. She made a face. "As for his crush—I don't think he ever really had one. I think you guys were wrong on that one. This is strictly a tutoring operation—has been, and always will be."

But next Friday night, Terry had just gotten out of the shower and was getting dressed to go to a movie with Rob when Sam came into the bedroom, looking worried.

"Terry, Brian's here," she said.

Terry looked up in surprise. "Brian? What does *he* want?"

"I don't know. Maybe you'd better come out and talk to him."

Terry looked at the clock. "Oh, no, Rob's going to be here any minute!" Hastily, she smoothed her hair and buttoned her blouse.

"Brian, I really can't talk, okay? I've got to be somewhere soon. What's up?" Terry asked as she walked into the living room.

"Oh, nothing special," Brian said, in a casual voice. He looked at her. "Hey, you look pretty tonight." He cleared his throat. "You're going out?"

"Well, yes, I am," Terry said uncomfortably. She'd gotten in trouble by lying to him once—she didn't want that to happen again.

Brian shoved his hands into his pockets and began to kick a crumpled piece of paper around with his sneaker. Terry couldn't see his face, but she suspected he wasn't too happy. "You going out with that guy I saw you with a few weeks back?" he asked.

Terry nodded mutely.

"I should've known," Brian said bitterly, still not looking up. "I guess it was dumb for me to, well, whatever." His voice trailed off.

Terry squared her shoulders. "Didn't you have a biology test today? How did it go?" she asked, as pleasantly as she could.

Brian laughed shortly. "Like it always does," he said, with a shrug of his shoulders. "Terrible. But I didn't come about that. I thought maybe we could—"

There was a knock on the door. Terry was too

tense to move, but when Sam opened the door, it was only Aaron, coming to pick up Sam for their date. In the noisy confusion of hellos, Brian slipped quietly out the door. Terry sighed with relief when she noticed he'd gone. It looked like his crush—or whatever it was—was back.

On Saturday morning, Terry and Sam went downstairs to do their laundry. "You know, Terry," Sam said, dumping a load of white clothes into the washer, "I think Brian needs to get some counseling. Seriously." She gave Terry a glance. "I really think he's in trouble. When we went to the movie last night, he was there, standing in line."

"Yeah?" Terry fed her quarters into the machine. "So?"

"So he started talking to this girl, giving her a hard time because he wanted her to sit with him in the movie. I think they knew each other, but she wasn't at all interested . Brian wouldn't give up, and he was being pretty loud and obnoxious."

Terry stared at her. "*Brian*? Brian Benson was being loud and obnoxious?"

"Yeah. After she flat out told him no, he just broke off in the middle of what he was saying and walked away, with his head down and his hands in his pockets. It was really kind of weird." She faced Terry. "That's why I think he needs some counseling. Psychological counseling."

Terry turned the dial to hot and began to pour in her soap. "I wish you hadn't told me," she said crossly.

"Why?"

"Because, I'm already worried about him. And I don't know what to do. I mean, I can't just walk up to him and say, 'Pardon me, Brian, but you're acting a little weird these days, don't you think it would be a good idea to go see a shrink?'"

"Come on, Terry," Sam said, frowning. "You're smart enough to know that's not the only approach." She went to the soft drink machine and got a diet cola. "Anyway, the direct approach might actually be the right way to go about it. The way we did with Stacy last semester."

"With Stacy?" Terry asked.

"Yeah, don't you remember that talk we had right after Thanksgiving?" Sam hoisted herself up onto the folding table and began to swing her legs back and forth like a little kid. "I mean, if we hadn't just come straight out and said, 'Stacy, don't you think you've got an eating problem?' she might have gone on trying to cover it up forever. And covering things up only makes them worse, in the long run. Look at her now—in a lot of ways, she's still the same old Stacy, but at least she's eating pretty regularly and she's gained some weight without going all to pieces over it."

Terry sighed. "You're right, I guess," she admitted. "I suppose I ought to talk to him about it. But the thing is that I just don't want to think about Brian's problems all the time. I'm helping him with his schoolwork—isn't that enough? I've got so many other, *good* things on my mind, that dealing with Brian's constant problems is a real downer. I don't have time for him, either. If I spend all my time helping him, I'll end up doing poorly in *my* classes. I can't do that." She hesitated. "Sometimes I sort of wish he'd go away and leave me alone. I know it's a horrible thing to say."

"I can understand how you feel," Sam said, sipping her soda. "But the fact is that Brian's problems aren't going to go away by themselves. Something is really bothering him, Terry, and sooner or later, you're going to have to deal with it."

Sam was right, but Terry had to deal with it sooner than either or them expected. It was the middle of the night when she woke up.

"What?" Terry sat up in bed. "What was that?" she asked Roni. "Did you hear anything?"

"Hunh?" Roni turned over sleepily. "Yeah, I did. Sounded like rocks against the window."

"That's what I thought, too," Terry said. She looked at the fluorescent dial of the clock beside her bed. "It's three A.M.," she said with a moan. Another rock hit the window and she reached for her robe. "What the heck's going on out there? Do you think Sam or Stacy forgot their key to the suite? I hope they don't break the window."

"Mmmf," Roni said, and rolled over again.

Terry went to the window, opened it, and looked out. There was no moon, but she could barely make out the hunched-over figure standing in the shadows below their balcony. "Who's there?" she asked timidly, shivering in the chilly nighttime breeze. "Stacy, is that you?"

"No, it's not Stacy," a husky voice replied. "Guess again." The person stood up straighter. "I'll give you a hint: I've got the lowest GPA in the freshman class."

"Brian? That's not funny. What in the world do you think you're doing, waking people up at this hour?" Terry's eyes were getting used to the dark, and she could almost see his face. "What kind of a joke is this, anyway?"

"Terry, is that Brian?" Roni asked, peeking out from under her covers. "Why is he throwing rocks at the window? How come he doesn't just use the phone, like normal people."

From below, Brian looked up at Terry with a pleading look in his eyes. "It's no joke," he said darkly. "Get dressed and come downstairs. I have to talk to you."

"What's the matter? What's going on?" Terry asked firmly. "Whatever it is, can't it wait until morning, when I'm awake? For goodness sake, Brian, it's the middle of the night."

The window of the suite next door opened and Terry's neighbor Janette stuck her head out. "What's going on?" she asked sleepily. "Who's throwing rocks? Did somebody get locked out?"

"Nobody's locked out," Terry said, embarrassed. "It's just this friend of mine, that's all. He's playing a little game. Sorry we woke you up."

"Oh," Janette said. "Well, tell him to be quiet, why don't you?" She pulled her head back inside and slammed the window shut.

Brian cleared his throat. "Terry, I'm telling you,

I'm not playing games," he insisted. "I *have* to talk to you. It can't wait." There was a tone of near desperation in his voice. "Look, if you won't come down, I'll come up." Without waiting for a reply, he caught hold of the drainpipe that ran up the wall to the roof, beside the balcony, and began to climb.

"Brian, that's crazy!" Terry exclaimed. "Don't do that! Get off that drainpipe! You'll get hurt!"

But Brian was already halfway up the drainpipe, climbing hand over hand, like a mountain climber on a rope. "I'll be right there. Don't worry, I know what I'm doing."

"Don't worry!" Terry cried. She drew her head back inside and shut the window firmly.

"Terry, what's happening out there?" Roni asked, sitting up straight, her eyes wide-awake now. "What's Brian up to?"

"He's almost up to our room! He's climbing up the drainpipe." She shook her head angrily. "Go back to sleep. He's just trying to get attention, that's all. He's probably just sick of studying or he's overworked or something and he thought it would be fun to come over here and terrorize us. I can't believe him, I try so—"

"Terry, calm down, okay? We'll deal with this."

Outside on the balcony, Brian began to bang on the window. "Let me in, Terry. I have to see you."

"Calm down? Think of something, *fast*," Terry ordered Roni.

"You can't come in here, Brian." Roni called in a loud voice. "I don't have any clothes on."

"Why'd you say *that*?" Terry whispered.

"Maybe he won't come in if I'm indecent," Roni whispered back. "He seems like that kind of boy." Terry rolled her eyes.

There wasn't any more noise coming from the balcony. "Brian," Terry said after a moment, "do you have any idea how ridiculous you're being? I am absolutely *not* going to let you in. Why don't you go home and go back to bed, and let us do the same."

"No. Not until you come out here," Brian demanded.

"Don't be stupid. I'm not coming out on the balcony. It's out of the question." She looked at the clock. "It's three-oh-five. I'm going back to bed."

There was another silence. "If you don't come out now," Brian said in a low, flat voice, "I'm going to jump."

"Jump? Brian, did you say 'jump'?"

"You heard what I said. I'm *serious*, Terry."

"Roni, I don't think he's joking," Terry whispered. She was getting very nervous about the whole situation. "What should I do?"

Roni ducked down into her bed and pulled the blanket over her head. "Let him jump," she said in a muffled voice. "After all, this is only the second floor. He couldn't do much worse than sprain an ankle."

"Come on, Roni, be serious. He can't jump," Terry said distractedly. "He'll hurt himself."

With a sigh, Roni sat up and rubbed her temples with her fingers. "Well, then, we could call Campus Security. They'd know what to do with him."

"No, I can't do that," Terry said, trying to think

of a plan and stay calm at the same time. "He's already on probation. If he was having other problems, too, the dean might decide he wasn't worth keeping at Hawthorne."

"So what are you going to do?" Roni asked.

"Terry, are you coming out?" Brian demanded through the window. "Or do I jump?"

"Hold on," Terry called. "Wait till I find my slippers—I'm coming. Don't jump!"

Chapter 9

"What is it?" Sam said sleepily, standing in her open bedroom door, rubbing her eyes. "I heard people talking. Is something wrong? Or did I just dream all that?"

Terry took her jacket out of the closet and pulled it on over her robe and pajamas. "I wish it were a dream. It's Brian," she said tersely. "He's out on the balcony."

Sam's eyes flew open. "What's he doing on the balcony at this hour of the night?"

Stacy appeared in the doorway behind Sam. "Who's on the balcony? Is there a fire or something?"

"No, there's no fire," Roni said, lounging against her bedroom door. "Brian's threatening to jump off the balcony, that's all."

Terry started toward the French doors that

opened onto the balcony. "At first I thought it was a joke," she said. "Now I think he's serious."

"What are you going to do? Shouldn't we call Security?" Sam asked worriedly. "Or at least wake Pam up?"

Terry looked at the three of them. She wasn't sure she knew what to do, but she knew she had to do *something*. "Sam, why don't you start a pot of coffee," she said, "And make it plenty strong. I'll go outside with Brian."

"If you need help," Stacy said, "all you have to do is yell and we'll come right out."

"Right," Roni agreed. "We'll stay up and listen in case you need us."

"Thanks," Terry said gratefully. "Well, here goes." She opened the French doors and stepped out.

Brian was sitting with his back to the wall, his head hunched down, his forehead resting on his knees. He looked as if he were asleep, but his head jerked up when Terry came out.

"Took you long enough," he growled sulkily.

Terry sat down beside him, pulling her jacket close around her. The wind off the lake was chilly, and she couldn't help shivering. "So what's wrong, Brian? What's been going on?" she asked, making her voice sound as light as she could. "Why do you have to talk to me?"

"Because," Brian said. He didn't say anything else for a minute. "Because you're my friend." He reached for her hand, leaning toward her. "You *are* my friend, aren't you?"

Terry squeezed his hand quickly and then pulled hers away as gently as she could. "Of course I'm your friend, Brian," she said patiently. "Who else but a friend—a good friend—would get out of bed at three in the morning to sit outside in the cold and talk?"

Brian considered that for a moment. "You're right," he said. "Then again, you're always right. Terry Honor Board Conklin, that's you. You've always got the answer." He laughed briefly, and there was a bitterness to his voice that set Terry's teeth on edge.

"Sure," he said, after another silence. "Who else but a friend would want to talk to me at three A.M. —or any other time, for that matter?" He laughed again. "You're a good friend," he said sadly, "and I'm sorry to bother you all the time. Truth is, you're the only good friend I've got."

"Hey, how about coming in and having a cup of coffee with me?" Terry suggested coaxingly. "We might even have something to eat lying around. You and I could sit on the sofa and talk. It's much warmer in there—it might make you feel better."

"Nah." Brian looked up at the stars, shining brightly in the clear, dark sky. "I've decided I like it out here. It's nice and quiet, and there's nobody bugging me. I don't like your roommates."

"Oh really?" Terry asked lightly. "What's wrong with my roommates?"

"They're too nosy, that's what. *All* roommates are

nosy," he added. "Mine's always snooping around, wanting to know how I feel, what I'm thinking. He never gives me a minute's peace." He looked at her and then moved clumsily to put his arm around her shoulders. "Hey, you're shivering. Let me warm you up a little. And anyway, we can't go in just yet. We haven't talked." He lowered his voice almost to a whisper. "I have to tell you something. In private. I don't want any nosy roommates listening to our conversation."

Terry leaned forward, trying to escape his hold. She heard Sam open the balcony door, and then there was a steaming pot of coffee and two cups sitting beside her. "Let's have coffee first," she said quietly, pouring. "Then talk. I have to be awake, don't I?" she laughed once, nervously, and handed him a cup.

Brian laughed. "Whatever you say." He moved his arm away from her shoulders to take the cup and gulped down half a cup with one swallow. Terry poured herself a cup and took a sip.

"So, did you really think I was going to jump?" he asked, sounding interested. "Were you really worried about me?"

"Yes, I *was* worried about you," Terry said honestly. "I've been worried about you for weeks." She took a deep breath. "You know, Brian, I've been thinking about the problems you've been having, and I think . . . well, I think maybe you ought to get some help."

"'Get some help'?" Brian set his cup down with a bang and ran his hand through his hair, standing it on end. "You're helping me, aren't you? I mean, we spend a lot of time studying together, don't we? So what other kind of help do I need?"

Terry cleared her throat. "No, not tutoring help," she said carefully. "I mean professional help. Like a counselor or something. Someone who can help you solve your problems so you can get a handle on your schoolwork. So you can start to enjoy life again."

Brian stared at her in the dim light, his eyes narrowing. His mouth tightened in a mocking twist. "Excuse me, but you're not trying to tell me you think I need a *shrink*, are you? Because if you are—"

"Well, not a shrink, exactly," Terry persisted, keeping her voice steady with an effort. "Just somebody—you know, somebody you can talk to. Like a counselor. Maybe somebody over at Student Life." She laughed a little and took another sip of coffee. Her teeth chattered against the edge of the cup. "You know, Brian, everybody needs help sometimes. I just want you to be happier. Talking to somebody who's trained to help people might be better. I'm only an amateur at this, you know."

"Yeah, well, I think you're all I need," Brian said, reaching for her hand again. "I've got you to talk to. You always make me feel better. Hey, I've got something to tell you."

Terry sighed. So much for her suggestion about counseling. Brian wasn't even going to consider it. "Okay," she said in a resigned voice, "what is it?"

There was a silence, and then Brian spoke, very quietly. "I love you."

Terry gulped. "Oh, Brian."

Brian's eyes glinted behind his glasses. "Yeah, yeah, I know. You've got somebody else. Rob somebody, that guy you hang out with all the time. And I don't intend to get in the way—I promise. I'm not that kind of guy. But I just thought"—he gestured vaguely and looked out across the lake—"I just thought maybe you'd like to know how I feel about you." Now that he'd said it, he seemed calmer and a little more relaxed—as if the only reason he'd come over to see her was to tell her that.

"I . . . I don't know what to say," Terry said, swallowing hard. She felt so guilty and so responsible for Brian's feelings that she didn't know what to do, either.

He turned and looked meaningfully into her eyes. "You don't have to say anything," he said, with a tiny half-smile. "I just wanted you to know, that's all." He paused. "Do you suppose," he asked, "do you suppose you'd mind an awful lot if I . . . well, if I kissed you?"

"Brian, I don't know if that's a good idea."

"Tell you what," he said, almost cheerfully. "If you'll let me kiss you, I'll leave and let you get back to bed. How about it? Deal?"

Terry nodded. His kiss was quick, as if he were embarrassed for having asked, and just wanted to get it over with. Then he stood up.

"I guess it's time for me to go. I think I've said everything I came to say."

Terry stood up, too. "I . . . uh . . ." She stopped mumbling and cleared her throat. "Well, if you're leaving, how about using the stairs this time?"

Brian glanced up. The light was on in the living room, and they could both hear voices inside. He shook his head.

"I don't want to see your roommates." He put his hand gently against her cheek. It was ice-cold. "Listen, Terry, I may not be the most romantic guy in the world, but I mean what I said a few minutes ago. I do. I really do."

Terry nodded. "Thanks, Brian," she said softly.

"Well," he said, "I just want you to remember, that's all. No matter what happens."

"I won't forget," Terry promised, swallowing hard. How could she?

"Good," Brian said. "See you later, okay?" And with that he swung over the edge of the balcony and disappeared into the darkness below.

Terry just stood on the balcony and stared after him for a few minutes before she went back inside.

In the living room, Terry's roommates clustered around her worriedly. "What in the world was that about?" Stacy demanded.

"Is he gone?" Sam asked.

"Yes," Terry said quietly. "Thank God. He . . . he went down the drainpipe. Same way he came up." Terry started giggling a little, then caught herself. The whole thing had been like a scene from a comedy—only it hadn't been funny at all.

"He didn't do anything weird, did he?" Roni asked. "We listened, but we didn't hear you call."

"No, he didn't hurt me, if that's what you mean," Terry said, shaking her head. It was warmer inside, but she was still shivering. "Is there any coffee left?"

Stacy went to get the pot while Sam went into the bedroom and brought back one of her mother's crocheted afghans, which she wrapped around Terry's shoulders. Terry sat down on the sofa and waited while Stacy poured her a cup of coffee. It wasn't very hot.

"Did you talk to him about getting help?" Sam asked.

Terry held the cup in both hands and took a gulp. Lukewarm as it was, the coffee warmed her a little. "Yeah, but he didn't seem to think much of the idea. He's really messed up, you know? It's painful to see him this way." Suddenly she put down the coffee, her hand shaking. A tear rolled down her cheek.

"It's all over now, Terry," Roni said soothingly, stroking her arm. "He's gone. You're safe."

"But that's . . . that's not what . . ." Terry stuttered.

"You're *sure* he didn't hurt you?" Roni asked worriedly.

"No," Terry cried. "Of course he didn't. That's not the problem. The problem is that he . . . he says he loves me!"

"I told you so!" Roni said triumphantly. Then she bit her lip. "Sorry," she muttered, "I shouldn't have said that."

"But you're right, Roni," Terry turned to her. "You were right all along, all three of you." She wiped her eyes with the sleeve of her robe. "I should have listened to you. Instead, I was so busy with everything that was happening in *my* life that I didn't pay any attention to the way *Brian* was feeling. And now it's too late. Now he's really going to be hurt!"

"Listen, Terry," Roni pointed out, "people fall in love all the time with people who don't love them back. They get hurt and for a while they think that life is all over. But they survive. It's not the end of the world for Brian. He'll get over it."

Terry stared at her. "But it's my fault—I led him on."

"No you didn't. Listen to Roni," Stacy said. "You didn't *intend* for Brian to fall in love with you. So stop taking responsibility for it. You can't take care of everybody in the whole world, you know."

Terry sat very still for a moment. Maybe Stacy was right. Maybe the best thing she could do for Brian would be to just cut things off entirely. He could find somebody else to help him with his homework, and she could get on with her life—and he could go on with his. And maybe find someone else who loved him back, the way she didn't. But she couldn't just never see him again, especially after what he'd said tonight. It would ruin his ego—and it was in pretty bad shape already.

"It must be nearly four," she said wearily. "I think I'll feel better if I get some more sleep."

"Tell you what," Stacy said, putting her arm around Terry's shoulders. "How about if we trade beds? If there's any more rock throwing tonight, you can sleep through it."

"Thanks, Stacy," Terry said, managing a weak smile, "but I can't start trying to hide out. That would only make things worse. Good night. And thanks, you guys."

"Any time," Sam said, smiling.

The next day, Terry and Rob stopped in at Mickey's for an ice-cream cone after a long and tiring Sunday-evening session at the theater. The production was only a couple of weeks away, and Eric was working them all pretty hard.

"Hi, Terry," Brian said. He was standing in line behind them.

Terry jumped, startled. "Oh, hi, Brian," she said, turning around quickly. She took a deep breath, studing Brian closely. He looked a lot better than he had the night before—much more cheerful, almost happy. She relaxed a little.

"Brian," she said, "I'd like you to meet Rob Goodman. Rob, this is my friend Brian Benson. We're studying pre-med together."

The two boys shook hands. "Excuse me," Brian said, "but do you mind if I talk to Terry for a minute or two?"

"No, not at all," Rob said. "Why don't you two go get a table, and I'll get the ice cream. We're having sundaes—what're you having, Brian?"

"Oh, nothing, thanks," Brian said sheepishly. "I just stopped because I saw Terry."

At the table, Brian leaned forward so he could talk confidentially. "Listen, Terry," he said, "I've been thinking about the way I behaved last night. To tell the truth, I'm really embarrassed about it. The last thing in the world I want is for you to get all mixed up with *my* problems. You're not responsible for what happens to me."

Terry tried to smile. "I want to help in any way I can, Brian. You know I—"

"I know you want to help," Brian said quickly. "And you have helped. A whole lot, already." He sat back with a smile. "In fact, you've helped so much that I think we can give up the tutoring sessions for a while."

"Give them up?"

"Yeah. Believe it or not, I think I've worked things out for myself. This morning, I was looking over all my notes, and, well, something just clicked. I think I'm going in the right direction now." He grinned. "And if I need help again, I know where to come for it, don't I?"

Terry looked at him closely, but his gaze was clear and unfaltering. "Are you sure you don't need any more help with your biology? What about chemistry?" she asked. "Midterms are coming up pretty soon, you know."

Brian nodded. "Yeah, I'm sure. Everything's under control." He stood up as Rob came toward the table with their sundaes. "In fact," he added, "I'm even considering your suggestion—about getting some counseling, I mean."

"Oh, yeah?" Terry said eagerly. "Hey, Brian, that's great!"

"Right. I'm sure that everything's going to be just fine from here on out. I feel like I hit rock bottom, and from now on things can only get better. 'It's always darkest just before the dawn.' Isn't that what they say?" Brian stepped aside to let Rob sit down. He looked from one to the other. "Well, have a good time," he said with a smile. He lifted his hand and gave them a little wave. "And thanks again, Terry. I'm sorry I had to get you out of bed last night. But it really did me a world of good. So I'll see you later—I'm on my way to the lab. No time like the present to get going, right?" He laughed and went out the door.

Rob looked after him curiously. "Get you out of bed?" he asked. "Are you two holding study sessions in the middle of the night?"

Terry blushed. "Well, not exactly," she said, sponing up the cherry on the top of her sundae. For a minute she hesitated, wondering how much she should tell Rob. But then she decided to tell him the whole story—before he heard it from someone else.

"Do you think he's serious about getting counseling?" Rob asked. "It sounds like he could really use it right now."

Terry considered. "Yes, I think he's serious. He looks so much better, and he seems really in charge of his life again."

"Well, that's good," Rob replied. "Maybe it sounds selfish, but I'm kind of glad that he's decided to cancel the tutoring sessions."

"Yeah, so am I," Terry agreed. "It'll give me another hour a day to cram for midterms. And believe me, I really *need* it."

Chapter 10

Midterms were scheduled for the second week of March. Unfortunately, *My Fair Lady* was going to begin its run shortly after midterms, which meant that Terry was, in Roni's picturesque phrase, up to her eyebrows in alligators. Also, there were several student music recitals for graduating seniors, and Terry had to don her Honor Board blazer and usher for three of them.

At the theater, Terry's area of responsibility seemed to be growing by leaps and bounds. "Tell Terry to take charge of it," Eric would tell Rob, about a particularly complicated problem. "She'll figure out what to do." When the costume designer, set director, or any of the actors had a question, Terry always knew the answer. The more she learned about the way the production was put together, the more everyone seemed to rely on her to get things done.

The production was quickly becoming the most interesting thing she did. The more she had to do, the more she seemed *able* to do. It didn't seem to bother her when Rob handed her still another assignment on top of the half dozen others she already had, or Eric ordered something important changed at the very last minute.

Her classes were going really well, too. Although she still didn't volunteer very often in class, she was getting mostly A's on all the quizzes or papers. It was very reassuring to discover that, when it was necessary, she could still be well organized and resourceful no matter how busy she got. With any luck at all, she'd manage another semester of good grades and be that much closer to med school.

When she opened her mailbox in the basement of Commons one morning and pulled out the envelope containing her midterm grades, she was thrilled—but not surprised—to see that she'd aced all her courses except comparative anatomy, in which she'd gotten a B. She went straight upstairs to the dining hall and, even though it was the middle of the morning, got a large piece of cheesecake and a glass of milk and took it to her favorite table, overlooking the lake.

"You're looking pretty pleased with yourself, Terry," Roni said, stopping beside the table with Stacy. Terry glanced up. "I'm celebrating," she said happily, holding up her milk in a toast. "To my future."

Stacy looked down at the envelope lying beside

Terry's plate. "Don't tell us," she said with a grin, "let us guess. All A's, huh?"

"All but anatomy," Terry said. "I got a B, but that's because I'm still working on the last dissection. I have to finish cutting up the cat first."

"Not to change the subject, but is that cheesecake?" Stacy asked, glancing down at Terry's plate. "I think I'll go get some." She went off in the direction of the dessert counter.

"Poor kitty," Roni said, "giving up his life to science." She plopped down in the chair, looking slightly glum. "How yukky. How do you deal with all that blood?"

"There's no blood," Terry said, shrugging her shoulders. "That's everybody's misconception. The animals we dissect have all been embalmed. There's no blood involved."

"Well, how about when you finally get to be a doctor? Isn't there blood involved with that?"

"Sure there is," Terry said, "especially if you're going to be a surgeon." She looked down at her cheesecake. "Uh, let's talk about something else. How did you do on your midterms?"

Roni sipped her tea. "About average," she said. "You know, mostly C's. Maybe a D or two."

"Hey, D's aren't average," Terry objected, concerned. "Don't you think . . . ?" She stopped, remembering what Stacy had said weeks ago about sounding like somebody's mother.

"It's no problem," Roni said. "Don't worry about it. *I'm* not." She leaned forward, her face growing more animated. "Hey, I've been thinking about what we ought to do for spring break. It's only a couple of weeks away. What would you think about going to Florida?"

"Florida?" Terry asked. "Where would we stay? How would we get there?"

Stacy came back with her cheesecake and a diet soda. "Did somebody say Florida?" she asked, pulling up a chair. "Who's going to Florida?"

"I thought maybe we could all go," Roni said with a smile, sitting back and watching their faces. "Over spring break. My folks have a time-share condominium arrangement and they've got some time coming up at a condo in Daytona Beach. It'd be just perfect for us."

Stacy raided her eyebrows, looking interested. "Daytona? That sounds great! I hear that Daytona has all the best spring-break parties."

Terry looked at her. "But what about Pete? Won't he be upset if you go away for a week?"

Stacy shrugged. "He might be. But he knows how claustrophobic this place can get sometimes. I'm sure he'd understand. It's not as if we're inseparable. Don't you think Florida would be great, Terry? Wouldn't you love to lie in the sun before the last push for finals?"

"I don't know. Yeah, I guess so." She finished the last of her cheesecake. "Except that the trip would probably cost a lot." Now that her major expenses were taken care of for the semester, she was managing to save some of her work-study money. But she wasn't sure she ought to blow it all on a spring-break trip. On the other hand, she didn't want to go home.

What would she do if she didn't go to Daytona with her roommates? She sighed. She should have been thinking about this weeks ago, but she'd been so busy with other things, she hadn't noticed spring break was practically here.

Roni waved her hand nonchalantly. "Listen, Terry, it won't cost anything except for gas and food. And we'll be splitting those expenses four ways. That won't cost much. You've got to spend money on food even if you stay here, don't you?" Roni could be practical when she wanted to, Terry thought—when it was for a good cause.

Terry glanced at her watch. "Oops! Time to go. Have you asked Sam about the trip yet?"

Roni shook her head. "Let's make our decision this weekend," she said. "If we can get everything firmed up, then I can go ahead and reserve the condo."

Terry nodded. The idea of a week on the beach sounded wonderful. She still had a few misgivings about how much it would cost, though, and then there was Rob. She would hate to be away from Rob for a whole week, even if it meant getting a good tan.

But when she told Rob about it Friday night, he thought it was a good idea.

"You need to get away for a while," he said, following her down the hall. They had just been to an Honor Board reception, and they were going back to the suite to make popcorn and talk for a while. "Anyway," he added, "I hear that Daytona's a terrific place for spring break. You'll have a lot of fun."

He grinned. "Hey, maybe I'll even come down for a couple of days and camp on your doorstep. I can always borrow my folks' van."

Terry raised her eyebrows. "Well, that puts a different light on it," she said, unlocking the door. "I'll think about it." The suite was empty. "Everybody must be out for the evening," she said, slipping out of her sweater and turning on the table lamp beside the sofa.

"Actually," Rob said, putting his hands on her hips and pulling her to him, "that was part of my plan for tonight."

"Your plan?"

He kissed her. "I bribed everybody to stay away. We haven't had enough time"—he kissed her again —"to ourselves lately."

"Oh?" Terry murmured, snuggling against him, hearing his heart beating.

He kissed the tip of her nose. "We see each other a lot because we work together, but we never have any time alone, to ourselves. Haven't you noticed that there's always somebody else around?" He sat down on the sofa and pulled her down next to him. "Getting in the way? A cast of thousands, so to speak?"

"Well, yes," Terry admitted, loving the way his hands felt, gently massaging her shoulders. She was breathing more quickly. She turned around to face him and ran her fingers through his dark hair, watching the light glint in his eyes. She could feel her own heart pounding now.

Rob leaned over and turned off the light. "But not

tonight," he said, moving his lips across her cheek. "Tonight there's just us, for a change. All by ourselves. Personally, I think we ought to take advantage of the situation."

Terry nodded. "I agree," she murmured. She was just losing herself in his kiss when the telephone rang.

"Don't answer it," Rob whispered, his mouth still against hers.

Terry turned her head away and reached for the phone, Rob's arms still around her. "I have to." She sighed. "I can't sit here and listen to the phone ringing for five minutes. It'll drive me crazy."

"You don't have to listen to it," Rob said. He reached for the plug and pulled it deftly out of the wall, then turned back to her. "See?" he said. "Now we can't hear a thing." He bent over and kissed her throat. "So what do you say to that?"

For a second, Terry wondered who had called and what happened when the plug was pulled. Did it just go on ringing on the other end or was there a busy signal? But then she gave up to the urgency of Rob's lips against hers and stopped thinking about everything and everyone else.

"M-m-m," she murmured, relaxing against him. "I can't say anything. I'm speechless."

"Good," Rob said, whispering against her ear. "Who needs to talk, anyway?"

Chapter 11

"Hey, who unplugged the phone?" Sam asked. It was around nine o'clock in the morning. She held up the telephone, it's plug dangling limply. "I tried to make a call just now, and there wasn't any dial tone."

Terry put down the book she was reading. "Oops," she said, coloring. "I guess that's my fault. It was ringing last night, and I didn't want to answer it so Rob pulled the plug. And then we . . . well, we got busy. I guess I forgot about it."

With a knowing grin, Sam plugged it in. "Got busy? I've got a pretty good idea of what *that* means." She turned around. "Hey, what do you think of Roni's idea about staying in that condo in Daytona Beach over spring break?"

"I think it sounds great," Terry said enthusiastically. "If I can afford it, that is."

"Well, that's better," Roni said, coming out of the bedroom yawning and stretching. She ruffled her hair with her hand. "Yesterday you sounded like you didn't think much of the idea."

"Yeah, but that was before I found out that Rob might be interested in going," Terry told her with a grin. "He says he might be able to drive down in his parents' van. If he did, he could camp out in it."

"Actually, he could stay with us if he wanted to," Roni offered. "The condo's big enough for at least eight people." She went to the coffeepot and poured herself a cup. "You could bring Aaron along if you felt like it, Sam. The more the merrier, I always say."

"That would be nice," Sam said, "but it looks like Aaron's going to New York over break." She paused. "In fact, I was even considering the possibility of going with him. But it would cost a lot, and I'm not sure it's a very good idea. Going to Daytona sounds better to me."

Roni took a sip of her coffee. "Well then," she said with satisfaction, "all we have to do is iron out the details, like when we're leaving and which condo we want to stay in. We've got our choice, you know. And then we'll have to decide what clothes to bring." She paused, looking thoughtful. "I think maybe I'll go shopping in Atlanta before we go. I really need some new—"

The phone rang. "I wonder how many calls we missed while the phone was out of commission," Sam said, picking it up. "Hello?" She held the receiver out to Terry. "For you."

"It must be Rob," Terry said happily, taking the phone. "We're going for a long hike this afternoon."

"No, it's not Rob," Sam said.

"Then it must be Brian," Roni said. "Hey, ask him how many drainpipes he's climbed lately." She snickered, grabbing for the phone. "Never mind, I'll ask him." She raised her voice. "Hey, Brian, how many—"

Sam pushed Roni away. "It's somebody named Alex," she said to Terry. "He's Brian's roommate."

"Hello, this is Terry."

The boy on the other end of the line cleared his throat. "Hi. We don't really know each other, Terry. But I live with Brian Benson, over in Baxter."

"Oh, hi, Alex." Why was Brian's roommate calling her? "What's up? What can I do for you?"

Alex cleared his throat again. His voice sounded a little shaky. "Uh, listen, I need to talk to you, Is it okay if I come over? Right away, I mean."

Terry sobered quickly. "Is it about Brian?" she asked. "Is he okay?"

"Well, uh, that's what I need to talk to you about," he said. There was something in his voice that made Terry suddenly feel uneasy, and the hair prickled at the back of her neck. "Listen, I don't want to do this over the phone. Would you mind if I came over now? I can be there in five minutes."

"Yeah, sure," Terry said. "It's okay. I'll be here." She put the phone back down slowly, with a troubled frown.

Sam looked at her. "Something wrong?"

"I don't know." Terry shook her head, still staring

at the phone. "Brian's roommate is coming over in a few minutes. He says he has to talk to me."

"Over here?" Roni asked. She stood up with a sigh. "Okay. I guess it was time for me to get going anyway. I've got a dance rehearsal this morning."

"Yeah, me too," Sam said quickly, starting for the door. "I've got to get to the library and get started on my research project." She grinned at Roni. "I want to have it finished before we go to Daytona."

"Hey, you guys don't have to leave just because of me," Terry protested. "I mean, whatever Alex has to say can't be *too* private. I've never even met the guy."

"That's okay," Roni said, disappearing into the bedroom. "I've really got to go to the dance studio."

Terry sat back down and looked out over the balcony, onto the lake. She hadn't heard from Brian in a while now, since the night they'd run into each other at Mickey's. She'd been so relieved that he thought he could handle things on his own. Obviously Brian was starting to take care of himself. And what he'd said that night on the balcony, about loving her—it was probably just some idea he'd gotten into his head, a kind of weekend crush. By now, he'd probably forgotten all about it.

The door opened. "Hey, Terry, something's going on over at Baxter," Sam said, beckoning excitedly. "Come and see."

"What are you talking about?" Terry asked, following her out into the hall. "What's going on? Is it a fire? It can't be, Alex just called from there."

"I don't know. When I came out into the hall, I noticed a bunch of people looking out the window down at the end of the hall, so I went to see what was happening. There's a bunch of campus security people and some Hawthorne Springs cops outside Baxter, and somebody said that an ambulance pulled away a few minutes ago."

"An ambulance?" Terry looked down toward the end of the hall, where a cluster of girls stood pressed against the window. Her hands felt clammy. "What do you suppose happened?"

"Is this suite 2C?" a boy asked tentatively, coming up to them. "Do you know where I can find Terry Conklin?"

"I'm Terry. Are you Alex?"

"Yeah." He looked at the crowd at the end of the hall. "Um, can we go inside?"

Terry opened the door, and they went inside. For a second, Sam hesitated, and then she came in, too.

Terry turned around to face Alex. There was a tight knot of fear in the pit of her stomach. "Alex," she whispered, "is there anything wrong?"

"I'm afraid so," he said miserably. "Maybe you'd better sit down."

Slowly, not taking her eyes off Alex's face, Terry backed up to the sofa and sat down. "What is it?" she whispered.

"It's Brian," Alex said. He swallowed. "He's . . . he's dead."

"Dead?" Terry blurted out, staring at him stupidly. "But how? Did he fall . . . was there an accident? Or a fire?"

Alex shook his head. "It wasn't an accident." He looked down at his hands. "Brian killed himself."

Stunned, Terry shut her eyes. "Killed himself?" she repeated weakly. "Brian Benson *killed* himself?"

"Oh, Terry," Sam murmured, sitting down beside her on the sofa and putting her arm around Terry's shoulders. "How awful!"

"Yeah." Alex cleared his throat. "I woke up an hour or so ago and found . . ." He looked at Terry closely. "Do you want to hear this? I mean, I don't have to tell you the details if you—"

"I want to know," Terry said, swallowing the lump that had risen in her throat. She clenched her hands tightly, trying not to lose control.

"Well, when I got up, he looked like he was asleep. I mean, he looked really calm and peaceful, so I didn't bother him. But then somebody called— somebody from one of his classes, I guess—and when I tried to wake him up, I . . . I couldn't." He fidgeted nervously with his watch. "He was already dead. He took an overdose of something—I don't know what yet, or where he got them. He left something for you—a note." He reached into his pocket and then handed the note to her.

Terry stared down at the torn-off piece of notebook paper Alex was holding out. "He wrote a note to me?" she whispered.

"Yeah. This isn't it, because the cops took the one that Brian wrote, and another one that he wrote to his folks. But I thought you ought to see this right away, so they let me copy it over for you. They said if you want the original, you can have it in a couple of days. After the investigation."

Terry's fingers felt stiff and wooden as she took the

paper. Suddenly her eyes blurred with tears, and she felt as if she were choking. "Thanks," she said, "for doing that."

Alex stood up awkwardly and thrust his hands into his pockets. "Well," he said, not looking at her. "Brian was a good guy, and I know he thought a lot of you. He used to talk about you a lot, anyway." He gave her a sideways glance. "He always said nice things about you, like how much you helped him and how much he liked you. But I'm sure you know that he hasn't been feeling on top of things for the past couple of weeks. It was like everything was just sort of piling up on him, and after he bombed his midterms he wouldn't talk to anybody at all."

Alex looked up. "Listen, Terry," he said, his voice beginning to break, "you shouldn't feel like this was your fault or anything. It wasn't anybody's fault. It just happened, that's all."

Terry clutched the note tightly. "Thanks for coming," she said.

"Yeah." Alex stood up and backed toward the door. "Well, if there's anything I can do, you know the phone number."

Terry nodded. "Yes," she said, "I know the phone number."

"Good-bye, Terry. I'm, well, I'm sorry." Alex shut the door quietly after he went out.

Sam stood up. "Coffee," she said, in a numb voice. "I'll make us some hot coffee."

Roni opened the bedroom door, her face white. "I'm sorry," she said. "The door was open a little, and I couldn't help hearing." She ran toward the sofa, where Terry was still sitting, clutching Brian's note. "Oh, Terry, I'm so sorry!" She looked down at the paper in Terry's hand. "Have you read it yet? What did he say?"

"Listen, Terry," Sam broke in hastily, "you don't have to tell us. Whatever it is, it's private between you."

The door burst open just then, and Stacy rushed into the room, wearing her jogging clothes. "Hey, what's this about Brian Benson?" she asked breathlessly, pulling off her green headband. "There's a bunch of kids hanging around the front door of Baxter, and one of them said that—" She stopped, staring at Terry. "Oh, my God," she whispered. "It's *true*?"

"It's true," Terry said tonelessly.

"Brian's roommate was just here," Sam told Stacy. "Brian left a note for Terry."

Terry unfolded the note and read it, her eyes moving slowly. It was only a few lines long, and by the time she finished, her eyes were so filled with tears that she couldn't even see it anymore.

"It's okay," she mumbled, thrusting the note into Roni's hands, "you can read it out loud if you want to."

"Are you sure?" Sam asked, bending over Terry, touching her arm gently.

Terry nodded mutely, and Roni began to read in a small choked voice. "'Terry, I just want you to know how much you've helped and what a good friend you've been. Without you, I couldn't have gotten this far, even. I know now that I'm never going to be a doctor. I'm not good enough to get into medical school. I know it's stupid to do this, but I can't think of anything else. I can't face my parents. I don't know what else to do with my life. Take care of yourself. Love, Brian.'"

Halfway through the note, Terry began to sob.

Chapter 12

Terry couldn't stop shaking. Stacy had wrapped her in an afghan and gotten her to lie down on her bed, and Sam had poured a mug of hot coffee with a shot of some kind of alcohol in it from a bottle Roni pulled out from under her bed. But she just couldn't get warm, and her hands shook as she tried to hold the mug steady.

"What do you think?" Stacy conferred with Roni worriedly, in a half whisper. "Should we call the infirmary? Maybe she ought to have a sedative or something. She looks like she's in shock."

"You might be right," Roni said, leaning over Terry and brushing the hair back from her forehead. "She seems awfully pale."

Terry shook her head without opening her eyes. "I'll be all right," she said dully. "I don't want a

133

doctor. A doctor couldn't do anything but give me something to help me sleep, and I don't want to sleep just now. I can't sleep."

Sam kneeled down beside the bed. "Do you want to talk?" she asked. "Maybe talking would help you sort things out."

Terry opened her eyes. "I guess the thing I don't understand," she said, "is why he was willing to kill himself for somebody *else's* dream. I mean, I can understand why he'd work night and day to become a doctor—almost kill himself with work, if that's what it took to get what he wanted. But he didn't *want* to be a doctor. It didn't mean that much to him." She began to sob again. "He was just doing it because it was a family tradition."

"Tradition runs pretty strong in some families," Roni said somberly. "His folks were probably putting an incredible amount of pressure on him, and he just couldn't deal with it anymore. He didn't know where to turn or what to do."

"If only I'd *been* there when he was thinking about this," Terry cried, "maybe I could've helped to change his mind."

"Listen, Terry," Sam said, "you can't let yourself think that. You heard what Alex said. It wasn't anybody's fault. Chances are that he wouldn't have listened to you, either."

But Terry didn't believe that. She pulled herself up on her elbows and sat staring wide-eyed at the others. "Do you suppose," she whispered, "that it was Brian on the phone last night? Do you think maybe he was the one who called, calling for help?"

She covered her face with her hands. "Oh, God, if only I'd answered it . . . I might have been able to help. If we could have talked, he might not have done it!"

Sam chewed on her lower lip. "I guess it might have been Brian," she admitted truthfully. "But you'll never know, Terry, so there's no sense in torturing yourself about it."

"It could have been one of *my* friends," Roni pointed out. "Or Sam's or Stacy's. And anyway, it might *not* have helped if you'd talked to him."

"Roni's right," Stacy said. "If somebody's determined to commit suicide, he's going to try it sooner or later, no matter who tries to stop him."

There was a knock on the outside door, and Sam went to answer it. In a minute she came back with Pam, their RA.

"I heard about what happened over at the Commons," Pam said to Sam in a low voice as they stood in the door. "How's Terry?"

"She's pretty upset right now," Sam said, "but she'll be okay in a little while."

"A little while," Terry thought. How long would it *really* take? How long had it been after David had died before she could sleep through the night without waking up in tears? How long would it be before she could think of Brian without wondering whether he had been sitting on the other end of the telephone line, listening to it ring over and over again, while she and Rob were lost in each other's kisses? She would always wonder whether she could have said or done something that would have changed his mind.

Pam came over and sat on the edge of the bed. "I know this is pretty hard to take, Terry," she said in a sympathetic voice. She looked around at the others. "It's good to have friends at a time like this. If there's anything I can do—"

"Why did he do it, Pam?" Terry burst out. "Why did this have to happen?"

Pam shrugged helplessly. "I'd be lying if I pretended to know the answer to that, Terry. It's just not a question that *anybody* can answer, even though you might be able to make a pretty good guess." She paused. "I know that you have to ask why, even though it hurts. And you'll probably keep on asking it for a long time, and keep on wondering whether you could have kept him from doing it—and maybe even whether you were responsible for it, in some way or other. It hurts, but we almost always keep on asking. Maybe someday the answer will come— maybe not."

Terry took a deep breath and looked up at Pam searchingly. "Do you think I *could* have kept him from doing it, Pam?" She swallowed. "If I'd been around to talk to him, I mean."

Pam picked up Terry's hand and turned it over in hers. "Maybe," she said honestly. "Yes, maybe *this* time you could have stopped him. Who can say what might have happened if Brian had been able to talk honestly about what was bothering him, to you or to somebody else?" She shook her head. "Yeah, you might have stopped him this once. But you couldn't be with him *all* the time, Terry, every day and every night. He's the one who had to figure things out;

nobody else could do it for him. Even though friends can try to help, they can't take total responsibility for the way somebody else chooses to live his life." She smiled wryly. "Sometimes it's tough enough just to take responsibility for *ourselves*."

Pam stood up. "Maybe it would be a good idea for you to get some sleep now," she said.

Terry nodded. "Thanks," she said. She sniffled. Her head felt achy and dull from crying, and her arms were so heavy she could barely lift them. "Thanks for coming."

There was a murmur of voices as Sam and Pam left the room. "I suppose his parents have been notified," Sam said.

"Yes," Pam replied. "They'll be here late tonight. Listen, if I can do anything, be sure and let me know. I'll be in my room studying for the rest of the day."

Brian's parents. In all this, Terry thought vaguely, as she drifted off to sleep, she hadn't even thought about Brian's mother and father as innocent victims —only as causes of Brian's death.

"Terry? Terry, are you awake?"

Terry opened her eyes. Rob was sitting on the floor beside the sofa. "Sort of," she said. She moved her head. The clock on the table beside her bed said two o'clock.

Rob reached for her hand. "I'm sorry. I came as soon as I heard. How are you feeling? Is there anything I can do?"

"Could you find out what time Brian's parents are

getting in?" she asked groggily. "And how long they'll be here? I want to talk to them."

Rob frowned. "Are you sure you ought to see them?" he asked. "I mean, it's only going to make things harder for you. What can you say?"

"I have to see them," Terry insisted. "I know it's going to be hard, and I don't have any idea what I'm going to say. But I have to see them."

"Well, okay," Rob said reluctantly. He stood up. "I'll check with Dean Peters. I'm sure he knows when they're getting in." He squeezed her hand. "Listen," he said, "how about if I come over later this afternoon and bring you something to eat? Would that be okay?"

Terry nodded. "Uh-hunh." She rolled over and closed her eyes. "That would be fine."

Terry met the Bensons in Dean Peters's office early Sunday morning. Her eyes were itchy and dry from lack of sleep, and her throat felt raw, as if she were coming down with a cold. The dean introduced them politely to one another and then left. Mrs. Benson was a tall, thin woman with soft brown hair. Her face was drawn and pale, and she had a tissue clenched firmly in one hand. Dr. Benson spoke with the air of somebody who was used to giving orders. He wore a pair of dark glasses, and his voice was quite gruff, considering the circumstances.

"So you're the girl Brian was studying with?" Dr. Benson asked brusquely.

Terry nodded and looked down at her hands, fingers twisted together. "I was until a couple of weeks ago," she said. She cleared her throat. "He . . . Brian worked awfully hard in all of his classes. That's what I came to tell you. It wasn't that he wasn't taking things seriously, or that he wasn't trying to be a good student. He really *wanted* to succeed. He knew how much you wanted him to be a doctor. He wanted to please you."

"But that's just what I don't understand," Dr. Benson said, shaking his head. He sounded a little angry at Brian—or was it at Terry? "Brian was a bright boy, intelligent, motivated. He did very well in high school. I don't know how he could have failed so badly in college. I just don't understand it." He got up out of his chair and began to pace back and forth in front of the desk, his face dark with anger and grief. "Somebody's got to be *responsible* for this change in him! Whatever it was, it's what made him fail."

Brian's mother reached out for his hand. "Don't, dear," she begged, in a choked voice. "Please don't. It won't do any good to go over it all again. You're just upsetting yourself."

Dr. Benson turned on his wife. "But he *did* fail, Elspeth. And that was what finally got to him, in the end. Not being able to accept failure. Remember how he moped around the house over Christmas, after he got his grades? He just couldn't hold up his head anymore, he couldn't face what was happening to him—maybe he didn't even know what had gone wrong. But *why* did he fail? *Why?* That's the one question we have to answer. That's what I came to Hawthorne to find out."

Mrs. Benson looked at Terry through tear-filled eyes. "Was it the pressure?" she asked. "I know Brian was under a lot of pressure at Hawthorne. Maybe it was his professors, pushing him too hard. Pre-med is really difficult, I know, and the professors have very high expectations. You're in the program, the dean says. Do the professors put a lot of pressure on you, too?"

"Yes, there's a lot of pressure," she said. "But mostly it comes from the students themselves. I mean, we all want to succeed, and we try very hard, just the way Brian did. We put pressure on ourselves, and we put pressure on one another." She swallowed, remembering how much pressure *she* had put on Brian to do well, to succeed. And almost as bad, she had assumed that their friendship was just a way of surviving pre-med, a means to an end. To Brian, it had meant more than that. She'd let him down.

Dr. Benson stopped pacing and pounded his closed fist against his hand. "I don't understand it now and I never will. Never."

Mrs. Benson tried to smile at Terry. "I know all this is difficult and terribly painful for you, too." She put her hand on Terry's arm. "And we do want to thank you for being such a wonderful friend to Brian. When he was home at Christmas he told us about the dance you went to together and what a good time he had. I think he mentioned you in almost every letter." She laughed a little. "He even told us about the night he climbed up to your balcony and you came out and the two of you sat and talked for a few hours. He said you were his best friend."

Terry's eyes filled with tears, thinking of that night on the balcony when Brian had told her he loved her. "Remember that," he said, "no matter what happens." His *best* friend. But his best friend wasn't there when he needed someone to talk to. His best friend hadn't truly understood what the friendship had meant to him. As long as she lived, she'd remember *that*.

Sunday night, Rob and Terry went to a movie over on Grove Street together. They walked to the theater and back almost in silence, and Rob didn't even ask to come in. He said good night at the door, kissing her gently on the cheek. "Get some sleep," he said. "Things will look better in the morning, when the sun's shining."

Monday wasn't any better, though. Terry could hear the students around her whispering in every class she went to. She could feel curious eyes on her, watching her every move. Everywhere on campus, people were talking in hushed voices, standing in little groups. When she walked by, the talk would stop, and everyone would stare at her until she was out of sight. But some people were a little more sensitive. Three or four even came up to tell her how sorry they were to hear that Brian had died. One of them—a boy she recognized from one of the classes she and Brian had taken last semester—actually seemed to mean it.

"I wish I'd talked to him more," the boy said sincerely, not meeting Terry's eyes. "I didn't even know he was in trouble until it was too late."

The professors were talking about it, too. Her biology professor from first semester stopped her outside the chem lab and told her how sorry he was.

"I know that you and Brian studied together," he said. "I saw you in the lab several times, working side by side."

Terry nodded.

The professor stroked his jaw, frowning. "You know, Brian's homework was always good. I just don't understand why he didn't do better on tests. Sometimes I thought," he added, "that he was *trying* to fail. I thought maybe he didn't want to be in pre-med, that perhaps he'd decided he wasn't cut out to be a doctor, and failing was his way of getting out. Students—even extremely good students—do that occasionally." He shook his head sadly. "I intended several times to talk to him about it, but I got sidetracked by other things and never got the chance. I wish now I had. I should have *made* time for him. I really don't have any excuse."

"It probably wouldn't have helped," Terry said thoughtfully. She remembered how strongly she had encouraged Brian to stay in the program when he talked about dropping out. Now she could see that dropping out would have been a far better solution for Brian. If he had dropped out of college for a semester or two, he probably would have felt differently about things when he came back. He might have taken some time off, even risking his parents' disapproval, if she hadn't pushed him so hard to stay, to stick it out with her. And if he'd been able to get away from the pressure of homework and tests—just for a little while, even—he might still be alive. Maybe he'd even be doing something that *he* wanted to do.

That night, Terry was in bed when Roni came in after midnight, tiptoeing carefully.

"It's okay," Terry said. "You can turn on the light. I'm still awake."

"Oh, okay. I didn't want to wake you." Roni switched on the light over her bed and sat down. "How are you feeling?" she asked, looking at Terry. "Did your day go okay?"

Terry clasped her hands under her head and looked up at the ceiling. She'd been awake for a long time, thinking. "You know," she said quietly, "I'm beginning to wonder about this pre-med thing."

"Oh, yeah?" Roni propped her back against the head of her bed and brought her knees up to her chest. "Like what are you wondering?"

"Well, here we are, a whole bunch of us, working night and day just to get into a profession where we're supposed to take care of people. But in all our classes, nobody ever talks about *caring*." She thought of the biology professor who had spoken to her and the boy she and Brian had known. "And when we do talk about it," she added, "it's just to say that we're sorry we didn't care enough, or we cared too late." She closed her eyes. "I mean, isn't there something fundamentally wrong with a system that doesn't train you for the most important thing you're supposed to do?"

"When you put it that way, yeah, I guess there is,"

Roni said thoughtfully. "From what I know about pre-med, the emphasis is all on grades. Not on caring about people." She gave a little laugh. "In fact, it sometimes seems as if people are the *last* thing the program cares about. They work you to the bone. It's so unhealthy."

Terry nodded. Wearily, she pulled the pillow over her head. "It just seems like there ought to be a better way to do it," she muttered.

Roni turned out the light in five minutes or so, but Terry wasn't about to sleep. She had too much to think about.

Long after Roni's breathing had smoothed into a soft, regular rhythm, Terry lay awake, watching the shadows of the maple tree move across the walls of the room as the wind blew. Something had to change, she thought. Soon.

Chapter 13

Early Tuesday morning, Terry picked up a copy of the Hawthorne Springs *Herald* on her way to breakfast. On the bottom of the front page was a headline in small black letters—HAWTHORNE PRE-MED TAKES OWN LIFE—and a picture of Brian, with a fairly long story about him. Terry noticed that almost every student was carrying a copy of the paper, and lots of people were standing around reading it before class and in the halls.

In comparative anatomy, the girl next to her was reading the paper, too. She glanced up as Terry sat down noisily, still gasping for breath from sprinting up the stairs.

"I just read about this guy named Brian. You were good friends with him, weren't you?" she asked. "I'm really sorry. Are you okay?"

Terry nodded and started to take off her Honor Board blazer to put it on the back of her chair. She had worn it because she had a meeting that afternoon and she wouldn't have time to go home and change.

"Well, you know as well as I do that it's a rough program," the girl said.

"The roughest. Some kids can take it, some can't. I don't mean to sound too harsh, but we've got to face reality. The strong ones are the successful ones." She glanced at Terry's jacket. "I can see that you're one of the strong ones. You have to be to make Honor Board."

Terry looked at her sternly. "But doesn't it feel wrong to you sometimes, all this competition for grades? It's so cutthroat."

"Wrong?" The girl shrugged. "Well, sure, it's not the healthiest thing in the world. Some people are going to get hurt—the ones who can't make it. It's a little neurotic. But if I don't get all A's every semester, I'll never be able to get into a top-flight graduate school with a good research program. I'm just being practical. I have to look out for myself." She gestured toward the podium, where the lecturer was sorting his notes. "And you bet that all the professors know that, too. That's why they're always after us to work harder. If we do well, it reflects on them—and vice versa. Their reputations are at stake, too."

"But what happens to people in a system like this?" Terry asked. "I mean, I really *enjoy* studying —or at least, I used to." She sighed. "But I'm not even sure about that anymore. I feel I'm doing it only because I *have* to. I'm driven, but I don't even know what motivates me now. Fear of getting a B, I guess. That's pretty sad when you think about it."

Just then the professor tapped on the podium for the students' attention, and Terry hurriedly opened her notebook and took out her pencil. Like it or not, she still had to take notes.

"All right, let's get started," he said rapidly, in a loud voice. "Today we'll begin a close examination of the human heart."

That afternoon, Terry was sitting in the front row of the darkened theater watching the final dress rehearsal. Rob sat down beside her and draped his arm across the back of her chair.

"How are you feeling? You know, when we went out the other night, I didn't want to ask you about Brian's parents. But now that you've had a couple of days to think about it, are you glad that you talked to them?"

"Yes," Terry said. She shivered a little, remembering Mr. Benson's angry insinuations. "I mean, it wasn't very pleasant, but afterward, I understood things a little more clearly. I could see why Brian was worried about performing well in school. His dad seems extremely demanding."

"So that's what happened to Brian, you think?" Rob asked. "Pressure from his parents to be something he didn't want to be?"

The orchestra swung into "The Rain in Spain," and Terry stared at the stage, where Professor Higgins was transforming Eliza from a shabby flower girl into a great lady by teaching her how to talk properly.

"I guess so," she said. "He knew that they wouldn't be happy if he wasn't a doctor like everybody else in his family. But it wasn't just his parents; they were only a part of it. It was everybody, everything—including me."

Rob dropped his hand on to her shoulder. "You? you're not blaming yourself for this, are you?" he asked. "That's not right, either."

"It's not blame, exactly." Terry frowned. "Not now, anyway. When it first happened, I blamed myself for not being there when he needed me. For not telling people I was really worried about him, for not searching him out during those two weeks he dropped out of sight . . . for not answering the phone that night. But blaming people—even yourself—doesn't do any good. I don't think I'm blaming myself anymore. I just want to try to understand *why* it happened, that's all."

She paused, looking up at the stage. Eliza was singing, "The rain in Spain stays mainly on the plain," with beautifully accented A's. "You know," she said, "I used to love *My Fair Lady*. I thought it was terrific that Eliza could change her life just by changing the way she talked. It seemed like magic to me, especially because I wanted to believe that it could happen. But now I don't believe in it." She made a face. "I don't even like the play anymore."

"By George, she's got it!" Professor Higgins sang on the stage, doing a little jig to celebrate Eliza's successful lesson. "I think she's got it."

"That's okay," Rob said, squeezing her shoulder. "Everybody *always* hates the production for the last couple of weeks. It's a natural thing, when you put so much effort into making all the details turn out just right. You'll like it again, in a month or two."

"No. it's not that," Terry said, "it's something else. I just don't think that you can be transformed, even if you want to be. Or that you can change yourself, with just a little hard work. I'm just not sure I believe in Eliza's happy ending any longer. It's too easy. It just doesn't work in real life."

Rob looked at her intently. "What do you mean?"

She put the newspaper she was still carrying down on her lap, with Brian's picture staring up at her. "I mean, there's Brian, believing that he could be changed into a doctor simply by getting a few good grades. But even getting all A's wouldn't have been enough to make him into a doctor, because he didn't have the dedication to be one. He didn't really *want* to be one. You have to know that medicine's right for you, and that you're right for it—or you're just wasting your time. And your life."

"Is it right for you?" Rob asked, very quietly.

"I don't know," Terry said. She looked down at Brian's face. "I thought it was, but now I'm not so sure. Lately it's just become a nightmare. And I don't think it's worth it."

"Terry, are you serious? Do you really mean that?"

"Oh, I don't know, Rob. Honestly, I don't know *what* I mean."

*   *   *

At noon on Wednesday there was a memorial service for Brian in the college chapel, a small, beautiful church with stained-glass windows. The chapel stood in a grove of trees on one side of the campus. *What a beautiful setting for such a sad occasion*, Terry thought. It was crowded, and everyone was sitting with their heads bowed respectfully in the dim quiet, listening to the organ. The college chaplain began to read some verses from the Bible.

Sitting with Rob and her roommates, Terry closed her eyes and twisted her fingers. She had been to only one memorial service before: David's had been held in the medical school chapel. He'd always said he wanted to donate his body for scientific research if anything ever happened to him. He carried a donor card in his wallet. There was no coffin at this service, just a few arrangements of white flowers around the altar, as there were today, and some candles. Brian and David, David and Brian. Terry couldn't believe how different the two of them were: one living only to be a doctor, the other dying because he couldn't be anything but one.

Suddenly she couldn't stand being in the chapel for another minute. She hated the quiet, meaningful, comforting words. And she couldn't stand the smell of those flowers or the sight of the little candles. "Excuse me," she said to Rob, sitting next to her. "I have to go outside."

"I'll come, too," Rob said, getting up hurriedly.

"No, don't," she said. She pushed past him. "I'll be okay."

"You sure?"

She nodded and walked down the side aisle to the back of the chapel and out the door. Outside, the sun was shining brightly against the brilliant green of the grass, and it was almost like summer. Over by the lake, she could hear the sounds of tennis balls being whacked across the court and friends calling to one another on their way to the Commons. She spotted a bench not far away, under a tall pine tree, and she went to sit there, closing her eyes and holding her face up to the sun's warmth. Sitting here, she could pretend that nothing was wrong, nothing had changed in her life. Sitting in the sun, she felt healthy and vibrant again. She didn't have to think. She could forget everything for a while and let her mind go blank for a change.

"I thought you might want some company."

Terry's eyes flew open. Roni was perched beside her on the end of the bench.

"Yeah, thanks," she said, closing her eyes again and relaxing.

There was a brief silence. Both of them seemed so relieved to be out of the chapel that they didn't need to talk. Then Roni said, very softly, as if she were wondering out loud, "Why is it that we just can't tell our parents what *we* want to do with our lives?"

Terry looked at Roni in surprise. Her arms were crossed over the front of her blue wool blazer, and she was staring out across the lawn, not really looking at anything, just staring. Her mascara was smeared, and her eyes were uncharacteristically puffy.

"I was just thinking about Brian," Roni said. "I

mean, if he could have come out and *told* his parents how he was feeling, maybe this wouldn't have had to happen. But he couldn't bring himself to do it. Was it his fault for not being able to tell them, or their fault for not asking him?"

"I don't know." Terry shook her head, thinking about her own parents. "I guess maybe our parents aren't able to listen very well, or that's what we think, so we don't try to talk to them. Not talking to them makes them lose touch with us. And then we say they don't understand us because they never listen. But the truth is we haven't said anything. It's kind of a vicious circle." *But*, Terry thought to herself, *it wasn't that way with all parents*. Rob's parents seemed to be interested in hearing what he wanted to do without telling him how to do it.

"Yeah." Roni chewed on the corner of her lip. "It's a vicious circle all right. But how do you break it? Take my parents, for instance. They never listen to *my* side of things. They want me to go to school, get my diploma, marry somebody who will carry on my father's business, have two kids, and join the Junior League." She dug the toe of her shoe into the grass, digging up a dandelion. "I gave up trying to talk to them a long time ago. They'll never change their minds about me—they've already decided. And of course I never do what they want me to— that's part of the vicious circle, too. Whatever I do, it's never what they want."

Terry stole a quick look at her. In all the months she'd known Roni, she'd never seen her cry. Was she crying for Brian or for herself? Behind them, the chapel bell began to toll, and Terry stood up. Everybody would be coming out in a few minutes, and she didn't want to stick around to talk to them.

"Listen, will you tell Rob I'm going to skip rehearsal this afternoon?" she said. She'd never missed her work-study job before, but there was a first time for everything. She'd skipped all her classes this morning, too. Her professors knew what was going on, so it was okay. They knew she wasn't about to make a habit of it.

"Hey, where are you going?" Roni asked, getting up. "Do you want some company?"

"No, thanks. I just want to be alone. I hope you understand. I'm going for a long walk." Terry turned and walked away, quickly, before Roni or anyone else could follow her.

The lab was deserted. It was a little after three, and Terry could hardly remember where she'd spent the last several hours. She'd been walking, she knew that, but she wasn't sure where. She'd come back to the lab kind of unconsciously, as if she'd been drawn to it. This was the place where she could get her bearings, could concentrate on her work again. That was what she needed now, more than anything else. To put everything that had happened out of her mind, to lose herself in her work, in her books, the way she'd always done before.

She perched on a stool and looked around. She had grown to like the cool, impersonal feeling of the Anatomy lab, with its long white tables, stainless-steel sinks, microscopes, and trays of instruments and shelves of equipment. Everything was always neatly in place.

Suddenly Terry closed her eyes, remembering a dream she'd had that week. Brian had been standing behind her in a white lab coat. No, it wasn't Brian, it was David. He was asking her whether she really *was* cut out to be a doctor. *Was* she? She'd answered yes to that question two years ago, when she committed herself to fulfilling the dream of being a doctor— to fulfilling *David's* dream. She had vowed she would take over his dreams and make them come true in her own life, she would reach his goals for him.

And she *was* succeeding. David's dream was coming true, along with all her *own* dreams for herself! She'd come so far, from high school to Hawthorne College. From uncertain, insecure Terry, sweating every test grade, to Terry the Honor Board member, who was maintaining a straight-A average and taking the most difficult pre-med courses at Hawthorne. From hiding out in the costume room to carrying out a responsible job up front, working with the director. From never dating to a long-term relationship with someone as mature and wonderful as Rob Goodman.

She'd come so far, and she knew exactly where she was going—didn't she?

Chapter 14

When Terry walked up the grassy hill from the lake on her way back to the suite, she saw her roommates lying out on the new "Rogers Beach." They were stretched out in the hot afternoon sunshine on the slope under the balcony, bathing suits and all. Sam, with her wheat-colored hair piled on top of her head, was rubbing Stacy's shoulders with suntan lotion, and Roni, wearing a pair of black wraparound sunglasses, was looking at something that was spread out on the towel in front of her. Beach Boys music was blaring out of Roni's cassette deck. It looked as if Roni was studying, but when Terry got closer she saw what she was concentrating so hard on: it was a stack of brochures with pictures of condominiums overlooking white, sandy beaches dotted with palm trees.

Stacy shaded her eyes against the bright sun, looking up at Terry. "Where have you been? We've been worried sick about you. So has Rob—he's been calling every half hour or so."

"Did you have any lunch?" Sam asked. "I made you a tuna salad sandwich, just in case. It's in the refrigerator." She gestured toward a cooler. "And we've got plenty of soda and juice, if you want some."

Roni put down the map she was looking at. "Why don't you go put on your bathing suit, bring your sandwich down here, and eat it in the sun? You can help us figure out which of these condos we ought to take for spring break."

"Yeah," Stacy said, "you need to get your mind off your troubles, Terry. Just stop *thinking* for a change. A little color wouldn't hurt you, either. It feels *marvelous* out here."

Terry sighed. "You know," she said, beginning to smile, "I think I will. Stop thinking, I mean. Start tanning. I don't have to look like I study all the time, do I?"

"Definitely not. I think an afternoon in the sun is exactly what the doctor ordered," Roni said with a grin. "Now hurry up and get changed before the clouds come!"

Terry was adjusting the shoulder straps of her red bathing suit when the phone rang.

"Hey, Ter, how're you doing?" Rob asked. "I looked all over for you after the service. Roni said you'd gone for a walk."

"I'm okay," Terry said. Cradling the receiver

against her shoulder, she opened the refrigerator door and took out the sandwich Sam had made for her. "I'll be okay if I just keep busy," she said. "Sitting around thinking all the time doesn't do a whole lot for my sanity." Sitting around thinking, the way she had done in the lab today, was definitely *not* what she ought to be doing. It was just asking for trouble. Stacy was right—what she needed was to turn off her mind for a while.

"So you want to keep busy," Rob said casually. "Well, what about the party at Eric's tonight?"

"The party!" Terry exclaimed. "Gosh, I'd forgotten all about it. *My Fair Lady* was going to open on Friday, and the director had invited the stage staff over for dinner tonight, to thank them for all their hard work.

"I know you may not feel very much like going to a party, but I think it would be a good idea."

"No, I *do* feel like going," Terry said quickly. "I don't want to hang around here, and I sure don't want to go to the library or the lab or any place like that. It'd be nice to see you, too."

Rob sounded surprised. "Hey, that's terrific," he said. "I was afraid I was going to have to use some powerful persuasion on you. How about I come over at eight?"

"Great. I'll be ready," Terry said enthusiastically. Yes, she thought, as she put the phone down, a party was just what she needed.

"We heard the phone ring," Stacy said, as Terry spread out her towel on the grass and flopped down beside her. "Was that Rob, by any chance?"

"Yeah," Terry said. "The director's having everybody over tonight for dinner." She started to nibble on her sandwich.

The girls exchanged glances. "I hope you told him you're going," Sam said. "I think it'd be a great idea to get out, socialize a little."

"I wish *I* had a party to go to tonight," complained Stacy.

Terry rolled over on her stomach. "I'm psyched to go out." Rob's picking me up at eight. Hey Stacy, you know that white dress that you loaned Sam last semester—with the full skirt?"

"The one with the V-neck?" Stacy asked. "You want to borrow it?"

Terry nodded. "Do you mind?"

"No, not at all," Stacy said, breaking into a grin. "I think it's a terrific idea. In fact, I've got this new eye shadow that I think would look great on you, too. Do you want to try it out?"

Terry nodded. "Sure," she said. If she was going to have fun, she had to dress for the part, didn't she?

"Okay, everybody," Roni announced, "listen up. It's time for some *very* serious discussion."

Stacy and Sam sat up at attention and saluted Roni. They began to scribble notes on the backs of their hands with imaginary pencils. "Gee, Roni, don't make this *too* tough. Terry's trying not to think, remember?" Stacy teased.

Ignoring them, Roni held up three brochures. "We've got our choice of condos, so we have to decide which feature is most important to our happiness. First of all, would you rather stay in a condo a block from the beach, or have a swimming pool?"

Stacy made a face. "What a *rotten* choice," she groaned. "Can't we have one that's on the beach *with* a swimming pool?"

Roni shuffled the brochures. "You can't have everything in this world, Stacy. Our third choice has a sauna and a tennis court, but it's a half mile from the ocean."

Terry spoke up. "I vote for the one closest to the beach. Aren't all the parties on the beach? Isn't that where everything happens?"

Roni raised her eyebrows, a little surprised at Terry's sudden interest in parties. "Yeah, that's what I hear."

"I'm with Terry," Stacy said firmly. "She's got the right idea. We want to be where the *parties* are. Anyway, who cares about a swimming pool when we've got the ocean?"

Roni turned to Sam. "What do you think, Sam? A beach, a tennis court, or a swimming pool?"

"Whatever you guys want to do, it doesn't matter a lot to me," Sam said. "Actually, I'm still sort of thinking about going with Aaron." She sighed. "I've never been to New York, and I'd really like to see it."

"You mean," Stacy said in an ominous voice, "that we're *second* choice, after Aaron Goldberg?"

Roni heaved a dramatic sigh. "Bottom of the list again, no matter how hard we try."

Terry put her arm around Sam. "That's okay,

Sam," she said, comfortingly. "We understand. Boyfriends come first, everybody else comes after that."

"Hey, that's not true!" Sam said indignantly, sitting up straight. "It's not that you guys are second with me, not at all, you're—" Then she saw that they were teasing, and she grinned and threw up her hands. "Okay, you win. Let's take the condo on the beach."

"Does that mean you're going with us?" Roni asked, pushing her sunglasses back up on her nose. "You're actually giving up New York concrete for Florida sand?"

"Who wants to go to New York in April?" Sam said, with a careless wave of her hand. "It would probably rain all week, anyway."

Stacy turned to Terry. "Lie down and let me put some lotion on your back. We don't want you to burn your first day out. Listen, everybody, if we're going to Daytona, we've got to get serious about our tans. We can't go to the beach looking all washed-out."

"You know, I was thinking," Terry said, relaxing under the gentle touch of Stacy's fingers, "about maybe getting a perm before we go. What do you think? If I get a perm I can stop using curlers. And I won't have to worry about what my hair looks like after I go swimming." She closed her eyes, suddenly remembering Brian's face the first time he had seen her in curls. She'd been on her way to the Honor Board initiation—she'd never thought of how much it must have bothered Brian that she did so well. God, she'd been so insensitive.

Roni pushed her sunglasses back on top of her

head and turned to Stacy. "Gosh, Stacy," she said in a worried voice, "I must have been out in the sun too long. I thought I just heard Terry Conklin say that she was thinking of going to a hair salon and getting a *perm*."

Stacy shook her head. "Yeah, I heard it, too," she said. She picked up her soda can and frowned at it. "Maybe it's something we're drinking. Or maybe *this* Terry isn't *our* Terry. Maybe she's some sort of imposter."

Sam leaned over and put a hand on Terry's forehead. "Are you sure you're okay?" she asked with mock anxiety. "It's a little early in the season for sunstroke, but you can't be too careful, you know."

Terry sat up and clasped her arms around her knees. "Listen, I know it sounds strange, coming from me, but I just feel like I have to do something *different*. Do you know what I mean? I just feel like everything in my life is coming apart right now, and the more I think about it the worse it gets. Something silly like a perm would help get me out of this rut."

Sam reached for her hand and squeezed it lightly. "We know *exactly* what you mean, Ter. It's okay. Really, it is."

"You're talking to somebody who dyed her hair pink once, Stacy said. "I understand."

"How about Saturday?" Roni asked. "There's a place out at the mall where I got my hair done before Christmas. I think they did a good job. I could make an appointment for you."

"How about Friday?" Terry asked. "There's no rehearsal Friday afternoon, since the production begins Friday night. And it would be nice to have it done for the cast party."

Roni reached over and ruffled Terry's brown hair. "Okay," she said. "Friday it is."

After the director's dinner, Rob and Terry stood outside the door to her suite. Rob studied her closely, his brown eyes intent on hers. "Are you okay, Terry?" he asked.

"What do you mean?" Terry asked evasively, her eyes sliding away from his. She fumbled in her purse for her keys. "Sure, I'm okay."

"Are you *sure*?" he said. "You're not acting like yourself, exactly."

"Well maybe that's because I'm not quite sure who I am just now."

Rob brushed a tendril of hair off of Terry's eyes and kissed her lightly. She slipped her arms around his neck, leaning against him, feeling his warmth envelop her. He kissed her again.

"Well," he said in a thoughtful voice, after a minute, "I still love you. Whoever you are. That's one thing you don't ever have to question."

Terry hugged Rob tightly to her. "I don't know what I'd do without you. I'm sure I wouldn't like it, whatever it was."

"I didn't know this was going to be a group event," Terry told Stacy, as Roni squealed out of the parking lot. "Maybe we should have invited the rest of the second floor."

"We could have sold tickets," Roni said, and

laughed. She turned the corner on what seemed like two wheels, and Terry clung desperately to the door handle. Why couldn't Roni drive like an ordinary person?

"Or chances," Stacy said. "We could have sold chances, like in the lottery."

"Chances on what?" Terry asked.

"I don't know." Roni gave a careless shrug. "On the way it comes out. On whether or not you'll be able to show your face at Hawthorne again?"

Terry felt her hair. "You mean there's some doubt?" she asked apprehensively.

"Well, you may have to miss some classes, you know." Stacy grinned.

"It's okay, Terry," Sam said. "There's only one way it can come out: *curly.*" Everybody laughed.

"Gosh," Terry said, looking at the mirror, "it looks like I've been fluff dried!" Her brown hair was a mass of luxurious brown curls that framed her face.

"Well," Roni said, "you wanted to do something different with your life." She grinned. "It's *really* different."

"*Vive la différence!*" Stacy cheered, throwing her hands in the air dramatically. "Terry, you look *gorgeous!*"

"It's beautiful," Sam said. She examined her long, straight blond hair in the mirror. "Maybe I should . . ."

Terry grabbed her. "Don't even think about it," she said. "Just because *I'm* crazy, doesn't mean you have to be crazy, too."

* * *

Rob didn't think she was crazy when she walked into the theater a few hours before the show. "Hey, Terry, you look great!" he said, coming over to her with a wide grin on his face.

The evening was incredibly hectic after that, so hectic that Terry couldn't have thought about anything even if she had wanted to—and she didn't. She had to race from one backstage wing to the other with messages, props, and glasses of water. She located a lost script, somebody's misplaced shoe, and a chair that had vanished from its regular place on the stage. During the first two acts, she pinned up a torn hem in Eliza's ball gown, dusted last-minute face powder on Professor Higgins's mother, adjusted the professor's cravat, and retrieved somebody's forgotten top hat from the trunk of his car. Finally, Rob took her by the hand and they sneaked quietly down into the front row of seats to watch the final act.

"I've grown accustomed to her face," Professor Higgins sang on the stage, "she almost makes the day begin. . . ."

Rob leaned over and put his arm around Terry's shoulders. "It's okay to change your hair," he said into her ear. "But hang onto your face, okay? I'm getting kind of used to it."

Terry leaned back against Rob's shoulder and closed her eyes wearily, letting the music wash over her. She was tired, but still felt energetic, hearing and seeing how well the musical was going. She was very proud of the part she'd played in the production. Eliza's transformation was taking place with such wonderful energy and vitality that it was inspiring. *She*, Terry Conklin, had helped to create the illusion that held everyone in the theater—her included—spellbound. It was one of the most satisfying feelings she'd ever had: it felt even better than making Honor Board, because it came as a total surprise. And Terry wasn't just a pre-med student anymore—she had character, just like Eliza.

The cast party was held backstage: the actors and actresses, most of them still in costume, were laughing and shouting, singing bits of show tunes and doing little impromptu dances to celebrate the successful first night. Some were huddled together, discussing key parts of the show. Others had brought some party tapes and were clearing away a dance floor in the corner. Terry had ordered the food for the party—dozens of sandwiches, huge bowls of potato chips and dips, an enormous chocolate cake that said "Rave Reviews" in pink frosting on the top, six-packs of soda, and a keg of beer. The beer was on the honor system, as at all official Hawthorne parties: if you were twenty-one, you could drink it. But nobody usually checked IDs. Some people went by the rules, some didn't. It was up to you to take care of yourself.

"I'm going for a beer," Rob said, helping Terry set up one of the food tables. "Want a Coke?"

"Actually, what I'd really like is some champagne," Terry said with a grin, spreading a white paper cover over the table. "I feel like celebrating."

Rob gave her a hug. "Will you settle for a Sprite?" he asked.

Terry made a face at him and began to take sandwiches out of the boxes and put them on the plates. "I guess so," she sighed. "I'll just have to pretend."

Terry busied herself setting the table, nursing the Sprite Rob had gotten for her. But when she was finished, there was nothing more to do except to fill her plate and go sit down and eat. The director was talking to Rob about some details of the production that needed to be taken care of before the next night's show. Terry didn't want to bother them, so she wandered around for a while after she had eaten, saying hello to everybody. They were all having such a good time, laughing and dancing, still dressed in their costumes from the play. Terry had to smile, thinking what a contrast this relaxed, easygoing party was to the stiff, artificial formality of the Honor Board receptions. And how different the people in the theater program were from the pre-meds: these people obviously didn't spend all their time worrying about where and how to get their next A.

"Hey, Terry, want to dance?" It was Freddie, still dressed in his Ascot costume and smiling from ear to ear. As Terry took his hand, he said, "You know, I haven't gotten the chance to thank you yet."

"Thank me?" Terry asked. "For what?"

"Why, for everything you've done," Freddie said, surprised. He stepped back, took off his top hat, and gave her an elaborate bow. "For holding this whole production together. We couldn't have done it without you, you know."

For a second, Terry just stared at him. Then her

face broke into a smile. "Hey," she said, as he held out his arms again, "thanks for saying that."

After that, she danced with Professor Higgins and with the stage manager. Then she went to the edge of the room and sat on some piled-up boxes, thinking about things and watching people dance. Finally, Rob came to find her, and they went out onto the dance floor together.

"Having a good time?" he asked, smiling down at her.

Terry looked up at him. "Yes," she said. "But I'd kind of like to leave pretty soon. I've been thinking about some things, and I'd like to talk. Do you mind?"

Rob shook his head. "Of course not. It's nearly one, anyway."

Outside the Fine Arts Complex, the campus was almost deserted, except for a few couples walking arm-in-arm along the lighted paths. It was cool and very misty. The drifting fog gave the campus an eerie look.

Terry shivered and put her arm around Rob, not saying anything. It wasn't working, she knew. She couldn't stop herself from wondering and questioning. And the answer to all her questions led her closer to the truth: that she didn't have the answer. Not at all. She could put on the green Honor Board blazer, but that didn't mean that Honor Board was right for her. She could curl her hair and borrow Stacy's elegant clothes, but that wouldn't make her sophisticated. Those changes were as superficial as Eliza changing the way she talked. So far she hadn't gotten to the root of what was really bothering her. Finally Terry knew what that was—and what she'd have to do to change it.

"Rob," she said quietly, as they started across the bridge over Hawthorne Lake, "I'm going to drop out of school."

Chapter 15

Rob stared at Terry, his eyes wide with disbelief. "It's really that serious? Is it because of Brian?"

Terry nodded. "It's not just Brian," she said. She stopped and leaned over the railing of the bridge, watching the fog swirl along the bank, under the willows, where the ducks slept with their heads tucked under their wings. "I mean, I think I could have helped him more, and definitely could have been a better friend. But I couldn't be responsible for his life as well as my own. No, his suicide is just a part of what's bothering me."

"So what is it?" Rob asked.

"It's me." She picked up a twig and dropped it into the lake below, watching it disappear into the dark water. "I mean, it's the person I *thought* I was. The girl who was so proud of her good grades and her plan to be a doctor. I don't know what's happened to me." She took a deep breath and turned toward Rob. "But I do know one thing. I can't find out who I am as long as I stay here. I need an objective point of view. Hawthorne is too much a part of me, it's too close to me, like a script that I wrote. The worst thing is that it isn't even my script—the part about being a doctor, I mean. I think maybe that I just borrowed that from my brother—it was easier than making my own decision, and it seemed so noble to me at the time. I'm just not sure it's the right thing to do anymore."

"But that's just it," Rob reminded her. "You aren't sure." He put his hand over hers where it lay on the railing, and his fingers were nice and warm. "Wouldn't it be a good thing to just finish out the semester, and see how you feel at the end of it? Who knows? Something might happen that will help you get things straightened out."

Terry shook her head. "I'm afraid that if I stay, I might get even more confused," she said. "I need time to myself—like Brian. It would have been better if he'd gotten away and sorted things out, away from the pressure the program put on him. I think it would be better to go now—before I get to the point where I can't do *anything*."

Rob touched her cheek briefly, then drew his hand back. "Where would you go? What would you do?"

"I don't know. Back to Philadelphia, maybe. I can get a job there." She bit her lip. Philadelphia would not be the right place to go now. Her parents were so blinded by their own problems that they couldn't see hers. And Philadelphia was so far away from Rob. If she left now, would she ever see him again? On the other hand, until she figured out who she was and what she wanted, she could never have a really *good* relationship with Rob.

As if he had read what was in her mind, Rob said, "As far as I'm concerned, it won't matter where you are, Terry. Philadelphia, Hawthorne, wherever —you'll still be important to me."

"Yes, I know," Terry said shyly. 'I feel that way, too. About you, I mean."

Rob put his arm around her and they began to walk again. The fog curled up through the boards of the wooden bridge, around their ankles and knees. Up ahead, it completely shrouded the pine trees on the bank and hid the shadowy bulk of Rogers House, on the hill above them.

"Promise me one thing?" Rob said, as they walked.

"What's that?" Terry said guardedly.

"Don't burn any bridges until the beginning of the week, will you?"

Terry looked ahead, where the bridge disappeared into the swirling, shimmering bank of fog. She gave him a crooked grin. "It's sort of hard to burn bridges in this weather, isn't it?" she asked.

"You're going to do *what*?" Roni exclaimed, dropping her hair brush.

Sam's eyes opened wide, and she put her glass of milk down with a bang, slopping some of it onto the coffee table. "Terry, you *can't* be serious!" she cried.

Stacy closed her sketchbook. "Terry, dropping out isn't the answer," she said. "You've got to stick with it. You've just *got* to. If you run away now, you'll never resolve your problems."

Terry shook her head and sat down on the sofa next to Sam, pulling her old flannel plaid bathrobe around her. "I've thought and thought about this," she said, in a calm voice, "but it's kind of hard to explain." She'd been awake all night, thinking about it, and the more she thought, the more she felt that she was right.

She looked at Stacy. "I don't think I'm running away, Stacy. I know it sounds crazy, but I think I'm running *toward* something. I don't know what it is, but I feel that it's waiting for me. I think I'd be running away if I stayed here and just stuck my nose in my books. That would be avoiding the problem."

"But dropping out—in the *middle* of the semester?" Sam said in a concerned voice. "What will that do to your record? What about getting into medical school?"

Terry shook her head. "I'm not sure what it will do to my record. I have to talk to the dean and see what he says. But I have the feeling that if I stay, I won't be able to concentrate, and my grades will go down. If I leave now, when I'm in good standing, I can come back and take up where I left off—if that's what I decide to do." She laughed a little. "Getting into medical school is the least of my worries just now. I can't look that far forward into the future."

"But *why*?" Roni asked. "Is it Brian? Is that why you feel you have to do this?"

"Brian is a big part of it," Terry replied slowly. "I mean, he's made me think about what I want to do, who I want to be. Why I do what I do." She wrapped the tie of her robe nervously around her fingers. "I guess maybe in a way it was his failure that made me look at my own success, and see what it was costing me."

"Where are you going to go?" Sam asked.

"Back home, I guess," Terry replied.

"Back home?" Stacy echoed. "You mean, back to live with your parents?"

Terry sighed. "Well, that's the part I'm not very sure about," she confessed. "I guess I'll go home first, and then see what happens."

The phone rang, and Stacy reached for it. "Hello? It's Rob," she said, handing it to Terry.

"Hi, how are you feeling this morning?" he asked.

Terry laughed a little. "Still confused about things, I guess. But I'm clearer about the need to get away." She looked at her friends. "I was just talking it over with everybody."

"So you're determined to leave. Right away?" Rob said.

"Yeah, I mean," she added hastily, "I haven't told the dean yet or anything, but I was thinking about calling my folks today and telling them to expect me home sometime around the middle of the week."

"I've got another suggestion."

"Listen, Rob," Terry began, "if you're going to try to talk me out of—"

"No, nothing like that," Rob said impatiently. "Listen, will you?"

Terry relented. "I'm listening."

"I talked to my mom and dad this morning. I told them what you were thinking of doing, and they had an idea they wanted me to pass on to you." Rob paused. "Are you listening?"

"I'm here," Terry said.

"They wanted me to tell you that they've got a job for you, if you want it."

Terry was speechless for a moment. "Are you serious?"

"Yeah, they said they have a job opening at the studio."

"But what kind of a job?" Terry asked. "Am I qualified?"

"The same kind of thing you've been doing at the theater," Rob said. "Production assistant. You know. coordinating things. running errands, getting people to the right place at the right time. They really need somebody who's intelligent, well organized, and has a good mind for details. All the things you do best. You're a natural at it, and my parents want you to start as soon as possible. If you're sure this is what you want to do, that is."

For a minute, Terry just sat there, staring into space. "Who did you say this was? Santa Claus?"

"Just one of his elves." Rob chuckled. "So what do you think?"

"Can you give me . . . say, thirty seconds to decide?"

"Well, I guess so. One-thousand-one, one-thousand-two—"

"I'll take it!" Terry said.

"That's great. I think you're doing the right thing. I'll call my parents right away and give them the good news. They'll contact you later to work out the details. Okay?"

"More than okay," Terry said. "Rob?"

"Yeah?"

"I don't know how to thank you. I mean, this is really terrific."

"Yeah, well, it's kind of in *my* interests too, you know."

Terry blushed. "It is?"

"Well, sure. It's a lot easier to drive to Atlanta on weekends than to drive all the way to Philly, isn't it? Besides, I'll have my parents spying on you night and day. Night and day mind you."

"Thanks, Rob. You're the best. I'll call you later, okay?

"What," Roni demanded, Terry had hung up the phone, "was *that* all about?"

"I'm moving to Atlanta," Terry said, in a stunned voice. "I've got a job."

A week later, Terry was packing all her clothes into boxes and suitcases as fast as she could. Rob was picking her up in less than an hour—she could hardly believe it. She took her green Honor Board blazer out of the closet, covered it carefully with plastic, and hung it on the door.

"This is so hard to believe," Roni said, watching from her bed. "After all those hours you spent studying, just to give it up this way . . . what's the world coming to? If you can't study anymore, then I definitely can't. And don't tell me I should pick up where you left off, either!" She shook her head. "I'm really going to miss you, Ter. I mean, who'll complain about me playing the stereo too loud? Who'll remind me to take my vitamins every day?"

"Well," Terry said in her most motherly tone, "I could write a note and put it on the bathroom mirror." She folded up the gray sweater that Roni had given her and put it on top of the other things in her suitcase. "Or I could make a cassette tape of instructions and—"

"Roni?" Sam came into the bedroom. "Pam Mason just called. She wants to see you. Right away."

Roni scowled. "Did she say what it was about?"

Sam shook her head. "She just said for you to hurry, that's all. What's up?"

"Who knows?" Roni asked with an aggravated shrug, getting up off her bed. "Who cares, anyway? She probably just wants to lecture me again."

"Well, Sam said slowly, "you've got to see *her* side of things. I mean, RAs are supposed to make sure that everybody plays by the rules. And when people don't . . ."

"I know, I know," Roni snapped, pulling on her shoes. "Listen, don't *you* lecture me, Sam. I really don't need that right now."

"I know," Sam said softly. "I'm sorry. If there's anything I can do—"

But Roni was already out the door, slamming it shut behind her.

Terry stared after her. "What was that all about?"

Sam sighed and sat down on Roni's bed, pulling her knees up. "I wish I knew. From the tone of Pam's voice, I'd say that Roni's in trouble again." She shook her head. "Remember when she got caught decorating Pam's door with shaving cream just before Christmas? Pam promised that, the next time, she'd really throw the book at her."

Stacy came into the room and sat down beside Sam on the bed. "I just got off the phone with one of my friends from the sorority. It seems that Roni was doing some heavy-duty partying at the Beta house last night."

"Heavy-duty partying?" Terry asked, raising her eyebrows. "Like what?"

"Well," Stacy said, "she was the star of the show. According to my friend, around 3 A.M. she got up on the piano and did a little impromptu dancing. Not exactly suitable for mixed company. I mean, Elvis Presley barely moved his hips compared with Roni. The Betas loved it, of course. I guess Roni thought the whole thing was very funny." She looked at Sam and Terry. "I don't think it's so funny. She's going to give suite 2C a *horrible* reputation—if she hasn't already."

Sam stood up and folded her arms across her chest. "Listen, you guys," she said firmly, "I don't know about you, but I hate gossip. And I refuse to believe anything I hear about Roni these days, except from Roni herself. So if you want to talk about her, you go right ahead. Just leave me out of it."

Terry nodded. "Yeah, you're right," she said. "We really shouldn't talk about her behind her back. And anyway, we've got some really important things to talk about. Like when you're going to come to Atlanta and see me. I'm going to stay with the Goodmans for a while, but I'll probably get my own apartment next month, and I'll always have room for you guys—even if it means that some of us have to sleep on the floor."

"I still wish you were going with us to Daytona," Stacy said sadly. She walked over to the window and stared out across the lake. "It's not going to be the same without you, you know."

Terry went up to Stacy and put her arm around her shoulders. "I know." She sighed. "My life isn't going to be the same without *you* guys, either." She paused. "You know," she said thoughtfully, "now that things are pretty settled and now that I know I have a job in Atlanta, maybe I *could* go. I mean, I'll be able to come right back to a steady paycheck."

"Really?" Sam asked. "That would be great. It's not that far away, you know."

"Okay, you guys, you just convinced me. Daytona, here we come," Terry said, laughing.

Roni stalked into the bedroom, looking furious, and flung herself across her bed.

"That was fast," Sam remarked, with a cautioning look at Stacy and Terry.

"She's talking to somebody else right now," Roni said. "I have to go back later." She looked at Terry's suitcase and the boxes stacked all around the room. "Are you almost finished?"

"Almost finished," Terry said, pulling the spread off her bed and stuffing it into a plastic bag. "I'm just having a hard time believing that this is really the end." She sat down on her bed. "I'll miss this place."

Sam came over and sat beside her, putting her arm around Terry's shoulders. "It's not *the* end, Terry. It's just one ending—and another beginning. You know, as the speaker said at my high school commencement. You're the one who said this was the most important decision you've ever made. Trust your judgment. You know you're doing the right thing."

"Yeah, but I'll still miss you. I mean, y'all."

"Look," Roni said. "Atlanta isn't very far away, and after you get your apartment, we'll come and see you every couple of weeks. And we'll all be in Daytona together for spring break."

"And who knows?" Stacy said. "Maybe you'll find yourself back at Hawthorne after you've got all this sorted out, starting over again."

"Maybe," Terry agreed.

"Or maybe you'll be working for a major network," suggested Stacy. "Maybe you'll be in *front* of the camera. 'So, Ms. Conklin, tell us how you got your start in show business.'"

Roni joined in. "'Well, it all started in anatomy lab,' you'll say. 'And then there was that perm. I knew it was the start of something big.'"

Terry laughed and looked around the room at her friends. They'd all gone through more changes in one year than in the rest of their lives combined. She had no idea what would happen to her next—but then, neither did her friends. But they knew that they'd always be there for one another, no matter what.

There was a knock at the door.

"Well," said Terry, "I guess this is good-bye."

Here's a sneak preview of *Extra Credit*, book number four in the continuing ROOMMATES series from Ivy Books.

"Vacation at last! I'm so excited I can't stand it." Roni Davies shielded her eyes from the Florida sun, which was already strong although it was only nine-thirty in the morning. She turned to her roommates in the backseat.

"You know, you guys," Roni admitted, "I never thought we'd make it." She poked Stacy, who was driving, in the arm. "Don't miss our exit," she reminded her again. Stacy grimaced as she maneuvered her silver-gray Mercedes into the passing lane.

"Stace, I just saw the sign for our exit," Roni repeated.

"I know. We have time." Stacy grinned patiently. "And I know you'll give me plenty of warning."

Roni leaned back. They'd been driving more than five hours. "Am I the only one who's excited?" She couldn't believe how calm Stacy was.

Sam piped up from the backseat. "Of course we're excited. You don't think we'll let you have all the fun, do you, Roni?"

"The truth?" Roni pushed her coppery red hair away from her face and turned around. "I didn't think we'd make it here together. I thought Stacy would fly off to the Riviera or something, you'd spend the entire week on campus with Aaron, and Terry would be fixing up her new apartment. What a disaster! I could have ended up at home with my parents or something." She made a face. "Ugh, all that golf. Hanging out at the country club is their idea of a vacation."

Sam laughed. "Your parents can't be as bad as you make them out to be. Anyway, we all decided to follow your lead this time."

"My lead?" Roni looked mystified.

"Sure. Party all the time, fun in the sun—just your style, right?" Sam grinned devilishly.

Roni grinned back, then screamed, "Daytona Beach, next exit!" She whirled around in her seat. "Stacy, pull over or you'll miss it."

Roni reached for the steering wheel, but Stacy slapped at her hand. "Stop it. When I'm driving, I'll do the steering, okay? Just take it easy."

"But you missed the exit!"

"Have I made a mistake yet?" Coolly, Stacy accelerated and passed several cars. "There's another Daytona exit coming up."

In the backseat, Sam yawned and combed her fingers through her tousled, sun-bleached hair. "Take it easy, you two," she said good-naturedly. "I'll drive, if you want. It's my turn, anyway."

"No way," Stacy said in her best, upper-class

Boston accent. "I want to be at the wheel when we hit Daytona so I can make my grand entrance."

"Good. I'm too tired to see straight, anyway." Sam yawned, glancing at their fourth roommate, Terry, who was sound asleep on the seat beside her. "Terry's got the right idea. I wish I could nap like that."

"If you'd worked as hard as Terry did all semester, you'd be sleeping, too," Stacy said.

"All that work and now she's dropping out," Sam said, looking at Terry fondly. "It's kind of sad—our last trip together as roommates."

"And we're going to make every second count," Roni declared.

"Like starting off at the crack of dawn?" Stacy gave her a poisonous look. "Only farmers get up at four A.M."

"But we agreed," Roni protested. "Why waste a day traveling? This way, we won't miss a minute of sun."

"It sounded great until we actually had to do it," Stacy admitted, stifling a yawn. "Right now, I'd be glad to be back at school, sound asleep."

"You can sleep on the beach," Roni pointed out.

"I think I will." Stacy slowed down as she approached the exit ramp.

Roni felt a shiver of excitement run through her. Daytona Beach! No classes, no exams, no papers to write—nothing but fun and sun for two solid weeks. She could hardly wait. She wished Stacy would let her drive, not to steal away Stacy's "grand entrance," but just so she could feel in control of things, make everything happen even faster. She couldn't help saying, "Hurry, Stace."

Stacy winced at the nickname as she smoothly took a right turn onto a local street.

"Wait, you should have gone left!" Roni cried.

"Will you stop backseat driving?" Stacy warned, making another right turn.

"We should have gone left. I know it."

Sam peered out the window. "Hey, I think Roni's right. Don't our directions say left turns?"

"What's going on?" Terry suddenly piped up. "Where are we? I must have fallen asleep."

"Stacy's lost," Roni cried. "Pull over, okay? I want to check the map." Roni got out their crumpled set of directions, scanning the paper hurriedly. "I know it said to turn left."

"I know what I'm doing," Stacy protested. "Trust me. I got us this far, didn't I?"

"Yeah, but I still say you should have turned left back there," Roni insisted. "We'll never get to the beach now."

"Cut it out, you guys." Terry clapped her hands over her ears.

"Then tell Roni to leave me alone and let me drive," Stacy snapped.

Suddenly everyone was arguing at once, and Roni felt like putting her hands over her ears, too. But then she saw something that changed her mind. "Look, you guys," she yelled. "Look!"

Straight ahead was a strip of shimmering, turquoise-blue water. The ocean, at last!

"We're here! We're here!" Excitedly, Roni grabbed Stacy's arm and shook it hard.

"Fantastic," Sam and Terry yelled at once.

Roni gazed around her in delight. "Just look at those palm trees, and that gorgeous blue water. It's even better than I thought it would be."

"Take it easy. It's not exactly the Riviera," Stacy drawled.

Roni laughed. "Maybe not, but how many of those exotic beaches are wall-to-wall college boys?" Roni asked, beaming. "Daytona Beach, here I come! Now who's complaining about getting up at four so we could spend the day on the beach?"

She tugged Stacy's arm. "Hey, stop! There's a parking space. Quick, grab it before someone else does."

Stacy slammed on the brakes, and the car behind them stopped short, blasting its horn. Then it pulled around them.

Sam groaned loudly. "The excitement begins. Never a dull moment with Roni around."

Stacy craned her neck and looked down the street, then peered at Roni. "Why should I park here? I don't even see our motel."

"Who cares? We're practically *on* the beach, and I can't wait to start my tan. Who has the lotion, anyway?" Roni pulled up her cropped top to reveal a skimpy green bikini top, which nearly glowed against her pale skin. "I didn't want to waste time changing," she explained.

"Sometimes, Veronica, you are too much," Stacy said, pulling the Mercedes back into traffic.

Terry laughed and, reaching forward, hit Roni playfully with the pillow she'd been using for her nap. "I can't believe you! You never cease to amaze me," she said.

"Yes, and speaking of being 'too much,' Roni, sometimes your bikinis are too little," joked Sam.

"Say what you want to," Roni said archly, "but y'all know you're just jealous because I'm going to get tan first!"